THE SILVER DONKEY

WALKER
BOOKS

Books by Sonya Hartnett
for older readers

Stripes of the Sidestep Wolf
Surrender
Thursday's Child
What the Birds See

THE SILVER DONKEY
SONYA HARTNETT

illustrated by LAURA CARLIN

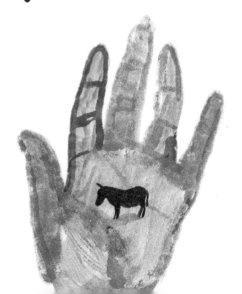

Published by arrangement with Penguin Books Australia Ltd

First published in Great Britain 2006 by Walker Books Ltd
87 Vauxhall Walk, London SE11 5HJ

2 4 6 8 10 9 7 5 3 1

Text © 2005 Sonya Hartnett
Illustrations © 2006 Laura Carlin

The right of Sonya Hartnett and Laura Carlin to be identified as author and illustrator respectively of this work has been asserted by them in accordance with the Copyright, Designs and Patents Act 1988

This book has been typeset in Giovanni

Printed in China

British Library Cataloguing in Publication Data:
a catalogue record for this book
is available from the British Library

ISBN-13: 978-1-84428-947-9
ISBN-10: 1-84428-947-8

www.walkerbooks.co.uk

For Leanne Marcuzzi
S. H.

For Dad
L. C.

CONTENTS

THE SOLDIER IN THE TREES

ONE cool spring morning in the woods close to the sea, two girls found a man curled up in the shade and, immediately guessing he must be dead, ran away shrieking delightedly, clutching each other's hands. As they ran they shouted to one another all sorts of horrors and secrets: "I think his ghost is chasing us!" screamed the elder; "I'm sorry I broke your dolly's arm!" howled the smaller one.

The elder stopped, jerking her sister to a halt. "I knew it was you who broke Villette's arm!" she cried. "You liar, you pretended you didn't! I've told you not to touch my things!"

The little girl clamped her mouth shut and wished she hadn't said anything. Her eyes glided up the slope down which they'd both just run. "The ghost might be coming!" she said hopefully.

Her sister, remembering the dead man, looked back the way they had come. The hill's brow was covered in thin birch and fat elms, and the grass sprinkled below the trees was long and brightly green. Now she'd caught her breath and recovered from the surprise, she realized it was thrilling to have discovered a dead man. No one at her school had ever found somebody dead; her brother, Pascal, certainly never had. He would be livid to hear of his sisters doing something so marvellous while he, the eldest child and only boy, had sat in front of the fireplace eating cinnamon toast. The older girl, whose name was Marcelle, imagined her brother's face when he heard the news. She brimmed suddenly with anticipation and glee.

… Although much depended, of course, on the man in the forest actually *being* dead. It would be embarrassing to fly home shouting that there was a dead man in the woods when the man was, in fact, only sleeping. And now she had caught her breath and begun to feel the cold, Marcelle reflected that the man had, indeed, looked equally asleep as dead.

There was nothing for it but to march back to the woods and have a closer look. The mystery must be solved. The facts must be set straight.

The smaller girl, whom everyone called Coco, squeaked when she realized where her sister was leading her. She dug her heels into the dirt. "Don't make me!" she whimpered. "I'm frightened!"

"You are not!" growled her sister, and Coco had to privately admit this was true. Nothing ever frightened her. "Besides, we must!" Marcelle commanded stoutly.

"What if Pascal finds him, and pretends he found him first?"

Coco knew that this mustn't happen. Pascal always spoiled everything. She hastened up the hill after her sister. In a moment, they were racing. The wet grass grabbed their shins and slicked their boots. They slid and stumbled on slimy stones. Their breath came out in cloudy puffs. They had forgotten completely their mother's request to pick an apronful of mushrooms to feed the pig. They giggled and clambered as fast as they could.

But as they reached the forest's edge, the sisters slowed from a run to a walk; and when the forest's grim shadow draped over them and the air became

grey and chilly with mist, they slowed from a walk to a creep. They lowered their feet carefully, trying not to make a sound. As they approached the hollow where the man lay, they were aggrieved to spy him sitting up. Clearly he was not dead. And although they had crept as quietly as they could, and kept themselves hidden behind tree trunks and weeds, the sharp-eared man must have heard – for he looked up from the fallen leaves, and stared directly at them.

MONSIEUR SHEPARD.

"**WHO'S** there?" cried the man, and then repeated it in a language that the sisters understood. "*Qui est là?* Who's there?"

He looked towards Marcelle and Coco and must have seen two skinny, flash-eyed little girls, wild as kittens born under stables, the taller dressed in her brother's hand-me-downs, the smaller rumpled as a street urchin – but then he looked to the mouldery soil and up into the trees, and behind himself towards the distant sea. He searched about frantically, as if the sisters were fleet butterflies and could alight anywhere. He scrambled backwards in the dirt, covering his knees in mud. "Who is there?" he asked again.

Marcelle and Coco stared. They had never met someone so frightened of them. They felt regretful, and sorry for him. "It's just us," said Marcelle. "No one else."

The man stopped scrabbling and became very still. He gazed towards a woodpigeon which perched above Marcelle's head. "I can't see you," he said nervously. "I'm blind. Who are you?"

That the man was blind was some compensation for his not being dead: Pascal had never found or even met a blind man. The girls, emboldened, peered more closely at their discovery, stepping from the shadows like fawns. They saw that the man had untidy brown hair and that his face was rather dirty. Coco, who had a sparrow's quick eyes, saw that he held something silver and enticing in his palm, something that twinkled and glimmered. Marcelle saw that, although he wore tatty old-man's clothes, the man himself was not very old – in fact he was young, as young as some of the fishermen's sons who raced small skiffs in the bay. His blue eyes shone and his cheeks were smudged with downy whiskers that the girls' father called baby-fluff. "I'm Marcelle," she told him. "I'm ten. This is my sister Coco. She's eight. Her real name is Thérèse, but everybody calls her Coco."

"Because I have hair like a black poodle's," explained Coco.

Marcelle felt compelled to expand on this. "When I was little and Coco was a baby and she had curly hair like a poodle's, Madame Courbet at the end of the road had a tiny black poodle named Coco, so that was the name I gave Thérèse – Coco."

"I see," said the man, huddling against a tree.

"And Coco – the poodle – got stolen," added Coco.

"Yes, she did, she got stolen. Everyone said Mademoiselle Bloom took her – Coco the poodle, I mean – because Coco disappeared exactly on the day Mademoiselle Bloom went to live in Paris, and she was always fond of Coco – the poodle, I mean – so everyone said that Mademoiselle Bloom was to blame. But that was a long time ago."

"When I was a baby," said Coco. "Coco would be old old old now – the dog."

"And now Madame Courbet doesn't have a dog at all," said Marcelle. "Not a poodle or a bulldog or a dachshund or anything. She says her heart is broken for Coco."

"But everyone still calls me Coco," Coco pointed out.

"Except when you're naughty or when something is very serious," her sister reminded her. "Then we call you Thérèse."

"Yes," admitted the little girl. "When I am in trouble, I'm Thérèse."

The young man turned his head from one sister to the other, following the voices as if they were birds. He wondered what to say. "That's a sad story, about the dog."

"Yes, it is," agreed Marcelle.

"Do you still have hair like a poodle's, Coco?"

"Oh, yes!"

The man nodded thoughtfully. "Then I know what it looks like, even though I can't see it."

Coco smiled deeply, and tugged at a ringlet. She was insufferably proud of her hair.

"What are you doing here, anyway?" asked Marcelle, wishing to change the subject.

A frown crossed the man's face. "I'm trying to go home. My brother is very ill. He is only eleven years old. His name is John. The doctors don't think he has long to live. My mother wrote saying that he wakes at night with a fever, calling out for me. She wrote that I should hurry home."

Marcelle and Coco were soft-hearted, and the man's

words caused their hearts to pang. "Where is your home?" asked Marcelle.

The man twisted on his knees, and pointed in the direction of the sea. "Across the Channel. Up the beach. Climb a narrow path between the rocks and walk three miles down a chalky road. When you reach a five-railed gate bordered on each side by oaks as big as churches, that's my home. You can see the chimneys from the road. John's window is on the ground floor, third from the right."

Marcelle considered. She knew that the Channel was very wide, and could be choppy and dangerous. She knew that three miles was a long distance to walk. "How will you get across the sea, up the path and along the chalky road?" she asked. "You're all alone. You're blind."

The man looked stricken. "Yes, I am."

"Are you a soldier?" asked Coco unexpectedly.

The man hunkered against the tree. "Why do you ask that?"

"Well, you are a bit like a soldier. You have a soldier's blanket and soldier's boots. And once there were soldiers who slept a night in our village and they spoke in a funny way, the same way that you do."

"It's called an accent," said Marcelle with superiority.

The man was fidgeting, casting his blind gaze about. The fascinating silver thing remained closed in his hand, gleamy as a fishhook, hidden as a jewel. He said, "I am a soldier – well, I used to be. I'm not one any more."

"Why not? Because you're blind?"

The soldier nodded wonkily. "That must be the reason."

"We could help you go home, Monsieur." Marcelle stepped a little nearer. "You must come with us to our house – we will each hold one of your hands, and guide you – and Papa will know how you can get home, I'm sure."

"No! No!" The soldier waved his arms. "You can't tell anyone about me – you mustn't!"

The sisters were startled, their eyes opened wide, but they were not afraid. Coco asked, "Why mustn't we?"

"Because… Why, because…" The soldier looked helpless, his hands dropped in his lap. "Because other people might not understand about John, and his being ill, and his calling for me feverishly at night. People might say I should go back to soldiering and forget about my brother, since he's only a boy, and sickly, and since there's a war being fought."

The soldier seemed badly worried, and was chewing his lip; Marcelle, who had noticed many injustices in the world, thought he was probably right about what other people would say. No one seemed to care about anything except the dreary war; nothing else appeared important any more. At any rate, it suited her to keep the soldier a secret: it felt nice to know something that Pascal did not. "Did you hear, Thérèse?" She addressed her sister imperiously. "Don't say a word to anybody. Not even to Mama or Papa."

"I shan't," swore Coco regally, lifting her chin.

"Maybe you should run home," sighed the soldier, his fingers shifting over the beguiling object in his hand: Coco craned on tiptoes but couldn't see it properly. "Maybe it would be best if you forgot about me."

Marcelle shook her head – there was no point having a secret if one promptly forgot about it. Then, recalling that the soldier couldn't see, she said, "We won't tell anyone – we promise, Monsieur! We can bring you food, and something to drink. We have to go to school today, but we could bring you something afterwards. Bread and jam, and some cognac or wine. Would you like that?"

In the past few days the soldier had eaten just a handful of biscuits and had drunk only dew; he was, as a result, parched and famished. The promise of a decent meal made him feel boneless and weak. "I am hungry," he admitted. "I would like something to eat."

"Then we'll bring it," said Marcelle. "Later – after school. You lie in the shade and rest, and wait for us to return."

The soldier wiped his grimy face and smiled. Already his stomach was rumbling. He leaned against the tree trunk, bundled up against the cold. "Remember, you must not tell anybody that I'm here. Not yet. Not yet."

"We'll remember," said Marcelle.

"What's your name?" asked Coco: her eyes were still fastened on the soldier's closed hand, on the slivers of silver that were glowing between his folded fingers.

"My name is Lieutenant," the soldier answered. "Lieutenant Shepard."

Coco thought "Lieutenant" was a strange name for a person to have, even a person with an accent hiding in the woods: but her mother often said there was no accounting for some people, so Coco dismissed the thing as unaccountable. There was something more important buzzing in her mind. She asked, "What have you got in your hand?"

The soldier turned his face in the direction of her voice. He did not reply immediately, as if judging whether some things weren't best kept to himself. The girls waited, tense as cats. Then the soldier unfurled his fingers and held up the thing that had hidden in his palm. The object caught the morning light and threw it sparkling into the trees. The girls drew a breath, their hearts leaping; they trampled quickly closer, scuffing up the leaves. There, on the soldier's palm, stood a shining silver donkey. It was small as a mouse, and just as perfect. Its legs were slender as twigs; it gazed through a fringe of carved lashes. It had four sturdy hooves, two fine, pointed ears, knobbly knees, a scruffy mane, and a smooth, rounded muzzle. Its waggly tail was tipped with a kink of silvery hair. It seemed ready to canter across the soldier's shoulder and

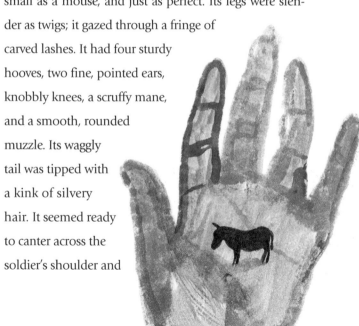

away into the forest. It was the most beautiful thing that Marcelle and Coco had ever seen. "Oh!" gasped Coco. "How darling! Can I have it?"

Her sister smacked her; the soldier only smiled. "I'm sorry, Coco," he said. "I need it, you see. It's my good-luck charm."

"Oh!" Coco's eyes felt melded to the exquisite thing. "And – is it? Is it lucky, Monsieur?"

The soldier's hand trembled as he stroked the donkey's back, but he was still smiling. "I think so, Coco," he replied. "I believe it is."

THE FOG

WHEN

Marcelle and Coco, having remembered that they were expected home with an apronful of mushrooms for the restless, pink-faced pig, had hurried away down the hill with many promises to return as soon as they could, the soldier dropped the silver donkey into his pocket and tucked his blanket around him. The forest air was cool and he was glad he had kept the blanket, though it was scratchy and smelled of dank earth. He was glad, too, for his army-issue boots and socks, which fitted comfortably and kept his feet dry. He knew he should have thrown away the blanket and boots, as he had thrown away his uniform and khaki pack. But he knew he would have been desolate without the friendly company of the blanket, and a man needs boots if he is to walk a long road home.

A man also needs his eyes, the soldier reminded himself.

Clouds had been gathering across his eyes for more than a week now. Before this, his sight had been sharp as a hawk's. The soldier had always thought blindness meant blackness, a never-ending, unbreachable barricade of inky nothing. His own blindness, though, was different. Rather than blackness, he saw white. Everything that surrounded him had been slowly bleached from view, like the words in a book left open in the sun; now only whiteness remained. It was as if his eyes had filled with a pea-soup fog and the entire world was hidden, now, within the whiteness, possible to touch, impossible to see.

When he had started out for home, walking resolutely away from the mud and bedlam of the war, he had carried a compass and been wearing his uniform and his vision had been clear. His first goal was the sea – if he could only reach the frothy waters of the Channel, he would feel he was almost home. He had walked and walked, one foot in front of the other, hardly daring to look up from the stony surface of the road. Carts drawn by mules passed him, and sad families without homes, and snaking lines of soldiers wafting the scent of mud and smoke. After two days he left the stony road, wary of being noticed – stopped – questioned. He kept instead to the rutted dirt roads which weaved and roamed past the fields. As soon as he saw his chance, he stole an old man's clothes which he found hanging on a line in the sun. Wearing these, the soldier buried his uniform. He slung his flask around his neck and stuffed his pockets with raisins; then left his haversack in a roadside furrow, weighted down with yellow pebbles. The blanket he hung around his shoulders. The silver donkey was in his breast pocket. The compass was in his hand. He thought of the sea, the rolling green waves. In the old man's clothing, he hardly looked like a soldier any more.

He did not talk to the few people he passed. He did not talk to himself. But in his mind he heard many voices – the roar of the generals, the singing of the soldiers, the crying of the wounded. Other sounds came to join these – the metallic rattle of barbed wire, the panicked whinnying of horses, the tat-tat of rifles, the scratter of exploding soil. Soon there was so much noise in his head that he did not hear the breeze or the heavy lowing of the cows or the chit of the red squirrels which lived in every tree. He was deaf to the geese that honked overhead, and to farmers who waved in salutation.

He'd paced along the road, head
down, frowning, chased by the sounds he was trying to
escape. There was one sound he listened for, however:
he strained his ears for the sigh of the sea.

At night he'd slept in barns and kennels, and one
night he slept in a cemetery, curled up with his blanket
between peaceful headstones. He woke to find the
world foggy; and although the cloud soon lifted from
the world, it stayed in his eyes, swilling like a genie
trapped in a bottle. Each day after this – each minute –
his eyesight became foggier. He threw away the compass when he couldn't see its quivering needle. He
walked faster – he hurried. He swallowed the last of the

water and did not notice when the empty flask slipped from his hand. Across the whiteness of his eyesight flashed flags of colour – the sage of uniforms, the gold of ammunition, the scarlet and purple of battlefields.

He listened, every fibre in him, for the hushed churning of the Channel; and shambled homeward as fast as he could, racing the incoming mist.

And when his eyesight was finally swamped and he could only sit in the woods doing nothing except hoping that the fog might miraculously clear, he knew he was close to the water – he could smell it, and, in the still of night, he could hear it. He supposed the shore lay less than a mile away. But for a blind man alone in a foreign country, a mile is a long, long way.

The soldier thought he'd been in the forest for two or three days before Marcelle and Coco found him, but time was mysterious in his cloudy world. Maybe he'd been here longer; maybe less. It felt like a long time – it felt like years. Long enough to become lonely, and afraid. In truth, even now, he was still lonely and

afraid – but the encounter with the girls had warmed him; their voices, which dashed along like brooks, had washed away some of the terrible clamour in his head. Knowing he wasn't alone any more made the soldier feel the way he'd felt when, as a boy, he'd woken to daylight on Christmas Day.

The Channel was surely just a mile from where he sat. He was hungry and shabby, but greatly cheered. The blanket against his face itched and smelled, but was warm. Across the Channel lay a cool green country, his home. Somewhere stood a gate with five rails and, beyond it, the great house where the soldier had been born. In the vast grassy grounds of the house he had learned to ride a pony and to skate on a frozen lake. Inside a shimmering glass-house at the side of the mansion, his father had grown an orange tree.

When the soldier was a boy, he had loved the house and garden and the bedroom that was his and contained his treasures. But when he was nine years old, and to his great dismay, he'd been sent to boarding school. He had hated it. He'd written letters begging his mother's permission to come home. Every day, at boarding school, he had thought of home exactly as he thought of it now, in the woods, years later: with the same heartwrenching ache.

He hadn't been allowed to leave boarding school – he'd been made to do what adults thought he should do, as children always are. It had seemed to take forever for him to grow old enough to be free again.

When war was declared he'd been quick to enlist, as had all his friends. When he was sent across the Channel to the muddy countries where war raged, he'd gone expecting to be amazed and excited. War, however, was nothing like he'd imagined. Instead of amazed, he'd been horrified. Instead of excited, he'd become home-sick and forlorn. Once again, he had hankered to flee.

This time, though, he hadn't bothered to beg any-one's permission to return home. This time he had simply turned and started walking, one foot in front of the other.

NORTH SEA
NGLAND
Yarmouth
SOUTHWOLD BAY
Harwich
Amst
HAGUE
Rotter
Helvoetsluys
BERGEN OP-ZOO
R. THAMES
LONDON
Deal
DOVER
Mardyk
Calais
Folkestone
Portsmouth
BEACHY HEAD
I. of Wight
Dieppe
HAVRE
Cherbourg
FRANCE
R. MEUSE

JAM AND MILK IN THE WOODS

MARCELLE and Coco were patient through their school lessons, and careful not to breathe a word about the soldier they'd found in the woods – although Marcelle could not resist asking her teacher, "How wide across is the Channel?"

The teacher, Madame Hugo, consulted her thickest book. "At its widest point the Channel is two hundred and forty kilometres."

c'est dans une l

"Oh!" said Marcelle, and felt boggled. Two hundred and forty kilometres was unimaginably far, maybe as far as the moon.

Madame Hugo was looking into the book. "At its narrowest point, however," she read, "the Channel is thirty-five kilometres wide. The water is *turbulent*, the wind is *westerly*, and howling gales are *very common*."

"How wide is it where we live, Madame? Very wide, or not so wide?"

Madame Hugo clicked her tongue: some of her pupils were clearly in need of further lecturing in geography. She unrolled a map of the world and jabbed at the microscopic dot which was their village. "You see that the Channel is narrow, where we live. Not much more than thirty-five kilometres wide. Which is fortunate, should you be planning to swim it, Marcelle."

The other children laughed, and pretended to be fish, and pretended to be Marcelle floundering in the wind-whipped waves. Marcelle ignored them. Thirty-five kilometres was much better than two hundred and forty. But it was still a long way. Not as far as the moon; but far.

It was a very slow day.

When Madame Hugo released the students, Marcelle and Coco hurried home. They felt nervous and excited and serious. "What if Mama says we can't go to the woods?" asked Coco in dread. "What if Papa wants our help around the house?" When they reached home, however, their father was at the dairy, bringing in the cows; their mother was ironing at the kitchen window, where a square of sunshine kept her warm. Their mother ironed the clothes of the village, but her own children ran carefree and creased. With their parents thus occupied, it was easy for the sisters to pack a treasure-trove of delicacies for their soldier. Coco even took a scrawny pillow from her bed.

Running out into the yard, skittish with the exhilaration of their confidential escapade, the girls were aghast to find their brother Pascal swinging on the gate. "Where are you two going?" he asked.

Coco slunk behind her sister, clutching her pillow. Marcelle scowled at Pascal. "Nowhere!" she said. "Nowhere interesting to you!"

Her brother snorted. "I already knew that."

"Climb off the gate, Pascal, we need to get past!"

Pascal stayed on the gate. "Why?"

Marcelle stamped a foot. "Why what?"

"Why do you need to get past?" Pascal drawled.

"We're going on a picnic." Coco peeked from behind her sister. "See, these are our picnic things." She tugged the satchel that Marcelle carried, and waved the pillow feebly.

"That's right!" agreed Marcelle. "We are going on a picnic. We're taking all our dolls. You can come too, Pascal, if you like."

Pascal snorted more wildly, screwing up his nose. "I don't want to go on a stupid picnic! Go away, I'm busy!"

"Busy! What are you doing, besides breaking the gate?"

Pascal drew himself up like a prince. "I'm waiting for Fabrice. He said I can ride in the sidecar down to the docks."

Marcelle and Coco clamped their mouths. They would dearly have loved a ride in the little sidecar bubble that zoomed like a rocket beside Fabrice's motorcycle. Naturally they did not tell their brother this. When he swung the gate open they stepped past him without a word, and walked briskly along the road towards the hills. "We can ride in the sidecar any old day," Marcelle told herself and her sister. "It's the soldier we must think about."

Coco slipped her hand into Marcelle's. The pillow bounced off her knees as she trotted on the road. Quietly she said, "What if he's not there?"

"I think he will be there," answered Marcelle, although she too was worried that, when they reached the hollow in the woods, they would find only leaves and feathers. Morning seemed such a long time ago, and the day had been so uneventful since then: she worried that the soldier was a dream that she and Coco had somehow shared. How disappointed she would be, if he turned out only a dream.

Coco knew she would cry if they found the hollow deserted, the silver donkey never to be seen again.

But when they reached the hollow in the shade of the elms, there he was. His eyes were shut, but he opened them. Across his lap lay a bulky branch, and he wrapped a hand around this. "*Qui est là?*" he called anxiously.

"It's us," said Marcelle. "It's Coco and Marcelle."

The soldier smiled with relief, and put aside the branch. The sisters came and sat close to him, crouching on the cool dirt. "I brought you a pillow," said Coco.

"I brought you some food," said Marcelle.

"May I see the silver donkey?" asked Coco.

The soldier reached into his pocket and drew out the silver donkey. It shone in his palm, its tiny ears upright. Coco hesitated. "I won't break it," she said.

"I know you won't. Thank you for the pillow."

Coco took the donkey and held it to her lips. It had a clear taste, like water. She loved this silver donkey more than anything in the world.

"Here's what we brought you." Marcelle was unpacking the satchel, setting everything out on the ground. "Some dried figs. A breadstick – my mother made it, I'm afraid it's very hard. A little knob of butter. Some blackberry jam. A jar of milk and some wine that Grand-père gave Mama when Coco was born. Here's a pair of Papa's woolly socks, and a scarf to keep your neck warm. Maybe you could wrap it around your ears too, if they're cold. So, what would you like to eat first?"

The soldier, though chilled to the marrow, lost, and blind, grinned into the trees. He thought he had never heard such a delectable rollcall of treats. "Blackberry jam is my favourite," he said. "I'll have jam and bread and wash it down with milk."

Marcelle busied herself preparing the banquet. She had forgotten to bring a knife to spread the jam. Coco pondered the silver donkey. Its surface was lightly scratched all over, suggesting a donkey's rough coat. She ran her fingers over the scratches, humming to herself. She did not hear the soldier ask, "Did you have a good day at school?"

"Oh yes," replied Marcelle. "But there is bad news, Monsieur. The Channel is thirty-five kilometres wide! You couldn't swim that far, even if you were not blind.

It could be worse – it could be two hundred and forty kilo- metres! – but thirty-five kilometres is still a long way."

"Yes." The soldier did not want to think about a sea that was too wide to swim. He had thought about that all day. Now he wanted to think about food.

Marcelle was spreading jam with a stick. She was glad the soldier couldn't see her doing so. Next time she would bring a knife. She said, "I've been trying and trying to think of how you might get home."

"Were you thinking of me, instead of your les- sons?"

"Yes," Marcelle admitted, "I was."

The soldier chuckled. "Well then, did you succeed? Did you think of a way for me to reach home?"

"No." Marcelle put the jammy bread in his hand. "I'm sorry," she said sorrowfully. "We're just little girls, Monsieur. I don't know if we're clever enough to think of a way for you to go home. I wish you had been found by smarter people, like Papa, or the Mayor."

The soldier ate the chunk of bread in two ravenous bites. He licked the crumbs from his fingers. He swallowed the milk in just one gulp, and sighed as if he'd drunk nectar. "Delicious!" he said.

"Was it?" Marcelle was pleased. "Really?"

"The Mayor could not have done better, Marcelle. I'm lucky it was you who found me, or I would never have eaten this jam and milk. Didn't I say the donkey was good luck, Coco?"

"Yes, you did!" marvelled Coco. "Did the donkey bring you here so we could find you?"

"It must have." The soldier felt around for more

food. Marcelle pushed the figs within his reach. "Even though I could hardly see, it's kept me safe and sound. Donkeys are clever and reliable like that. You can always trust a donkey."

"Monsieur Corto in the village has a donkey," said Coco. "It pulls the fish cart. But I wouldn't trust that donkey."

"Why not?"

"If you get too close, it bites."

The soldier crunched a fig. "Monsieur Corto must not treat his donkey well. Only unloved and mistreated donkeys bite. And why shouldn't they? No one likes to be unloved and mistreated. Donkeys that are loved don't bite – they kiss."

"Kiss!" shrieked Marcelle. "I would not like to be kissed by a donkey!"

"No, you would like to be kissed by Émile Rivère!"

Marcelle wheeled to her sister, shocked. "Oh! I would not! Shut up, Coco!"

The soldier asked, "Who is Émile Rivère?"

"A boy in our village!" crowed Coco. "Marcelle sits next to him in school! She loves him!"

"I do not!" bawled Marcelle. "Be quiet, Thérèse!"

"She wants to kiss him! One day she did!"

"I didn't! Go away, you're stupid!"

"I would rather be kissed by a donkey than kissed by a boy, especially Émile Rivère!"

The soldier was laughing, but kindly. "Be careful, Coco. One day you might change your mind about boys."

"I never will!"

"A donkey's kiss is different, anyway – nothing at all like a person's kiss."

"What is it like, then?" asked Marcelle, who was desperate to drop the subject of Émile.

The soldier dusted his hands and leaned back against the tree. Coco's pillow was bundled at his shoulders and the blanket was draped over him. He was warm and well-fed and no longer lonely: for now, he let himself forget that he was blind, and yearning to go home. The dreadful sounds of the battlefield, which tolled day and night in his mind, were quietened as if a truce had been called; for now, he was actually happy. He felt a nudging at his arm, and then the small weight of the silver donkey as Coco placed it in his hand. He felt the blunt points of its four legs standing on his palm. He reached for the last fig and, chewing it thoughtfully and in tiny pieces, told an old story.

THE FIRST TALE

THIS is the story.

One day, a long time ago, a mighty king decided to count all the people in his kingdom so he could remind himself, when he was bored, of how many people were poorer and less powerful than he. And to make things difficult, the king decreed that everyone must return, for the census, to the place where they'd been born.

Some people, over the years, had travelled far from where they'd been born, and, because cars and bicycles and motorcycles hadn't yet been invented, many of these people had to walk all the way back to their towns. One of them was a man named Joseph. He'd been born in a town called Bethlehem. Bethlehem was far from Nazareth, which was where Joseph now lived with his wife Mary. Between Bethlehem and Nazareth lay rocky, sandy, sun-soaked miles. For himself, Joseph did not mind the rocks and sand; but Mary was going to have a baby soon, and Joseph worried that the long walk to Bethlehem would be impossible for her. He did not know what to do. He couldn't carry Mary to Bethlehem. He was too poor to buy a mule and cart that could fetch her there. As the day of the great census drew nearer, Joseph worried frantically, and Mary's baby came closer to being born.

And then one morning Joseph woke to the hee-haw of his neighbour's donkey, and knew what he must do. He ran outside, across the spindly grass and thorns, and jumped the wall into his neighbour's yard. "Ruth!" he cried. "Where are you?"

Joseph's neighbour Ruth was an old lady. Her husband had died years ago and she lived with her finches and nanny-goats and her very ancient donkey, Hazel. "Hush that wailing, Joseph," she said. "You'll wake the dead."

Joseph clutched his hands together. "Ruth," he said, "I need your help. I need to borrow your donkey."

Ruth peered at him. "If you want to borrow my donkey," she said, "you must want a donkey's help, not mine. Why would you need my Hazel?"

"Mary and I must go to Bethlehem for the census," Joseph began. "Mary can't walk there. The baby is coming any day. The only way Mary will reach Bethlehem is if you let me borrow Hazel, and Hazel carries her."

Ruth looked Joseph up and down. She looked to where Hazel stood dozing in the sun. Hazel was a small grey donkey. When she was young she had been

pretty, nimble, and quick. Now she was aged as the mountains, bony and rickety. She had always been a kind animal, had always tried her best. Ruth had promised her donkey that when they both grew old, they would spend their days doing nothing but sleeping in the sun. Hazel was old now, and Ruth was keeping her promise. "Bethlehem is a long way from here," she said. "My Hazel is elderly, and growing weak."

"I know. But I would take good care of her, Ruth, I promise. Hazel is my only hope. If I don't get to Bethlehem for the census, who knows what the king will do? He might throw me in prison, and who would fend for Mary and the baby then?"

Ruth wrinkled her face. She knew what she would do, were the king to suddenly appear and start yabbering about prisons. She'd bend him over her knee and give him the tanning his mother should have given him when he was a boy. She hobbled across the yard to where Hazel stood, and whispered into the donkey's long ear. "Carry Mary safely to Bethlehem," she said. "Do your best, my Hazel. And then come home to me."

So Joseph, much relieved, led Hazel to his house, and soon he and Mary were on their way to Bethlehem. They remembered Joseph's promise to Ruth, and took good care of Hazel. They tried to find the flattest course between Nazareth and Bethlehem, so Hazel needn't walk up hills. They stopped in shade during the heat of the day, so Hazel wouldn't suffer in the sun. When they found a water well, Joseph filled a bucket for Hazel before taking a drink himself. If there was rubble or rocks on the path, Joseph pushed them aside. Mary, although she was tired and aching, climbed from Hazel and walked when she could, so the little grey donkey might rest from the burden of her weight.

Hazel did her best. She never stopped and refused to move. She never brayed noisily when Joseph was cat-napping in the shade. Her legs and back hurt, and the

sun was too bright for her eyes, but she kept walking at a steady pace. Flies buzzed round her broad grey face, and Mary used an olive switch to chase them away. Sometimes the donkey felt Mary's baby dancing, although the baby wasn't yet born. Steadily, steadily she walked, keeping the dancing baby safe, rocking him soothingly. At night, under the flickering stars, Joseph groomed burrs from Hazel's coat. "You're a good little donkey," he told her.

After four days of walking, they reached Bethlehem. Night was gathering, and the town was lit by the flames of countless lamps. As they passed between the tilting gates, Mary said, "Oh!"

Hazel's ears pricked up. "What is it?" asked Joseph.

"I think the baby will be born tonight," said Mary, and smiled.

"Then we must find a room, quickly!" cried Joseph,

who was flustered and excited. He didn't know anything about fatherhood. He tugged the lead rope, hurrying Hazel on. They stopped at the first inn they saw. "Please, may we hire a room?" Joseph asked the owner.

"No rooms!" said the owner. "The inn is booked out!"

"Oh well," said Mary. "We'll try the next inn."

"Please, may we hire a room?" said Joseph to the owner of the next inn.

"No rooms!" said the owner. "My inn is booked out."

"Are you sure?" asked Joseph. "We're desperate. My wife is having a baby tonight."

"Then I am definitely sure!" said the owner. "No babies may be born in my inn! Not tonight, not ever!" He slammed the door in Joseph's face.

"Oh dear," said Mary. "Let's try another inn, Joseph."

So Hazel, Mary and Joseph walked the crowded streets of Bethlehem until they reached another inn. It was a small, ramshackle building. Joseph would have liked his baby to be born in a palace, but he could only afford the most humble inns. "Please," he said to the owner, "may we have a room for the night?"

"No!" said the owner. "Bethlehem is full of travellers who've returned for the census. You won't find a vacancy at any inn in town. You've arrived too late, you see!"

Joseph's shoulders fell. "My wife is having a baby tonight," he sighed. "I don't know what we'll do."

The innkeeper looked at Mary, who stood quietly beside the old donkey. The innkeeper was a good man. He knew he must try to help. "Behind the inn is a stable," he said. "You're welcome to stay there. There's plenty of fresh straw to rest on, and you'll be sheltered and out of the wind. It is the best I can do."

A stable! This was even worse than a humble inn. How could Joseph tell his friends that his baby had been born in a stable? But Mary said to the innkeeper, "Thank you, we're grateful," and led Hazel around the corner of the building, to where the stable stood.

There was no lamp inside the stable, but it was a clear, starry evening and the three travellers could see by moonlight that the stable was occupied by two dun cows who stood sedately at the manger, and by three fat sheep who clustered in a corner and blinked their strange eyes at the newcomers. The heat of the animals had warmed the stables cosily. Mary sat down on a pile of straw. Joseph took the rug from Hazel's back and filled a feedbag with hay. Then he set about making a meal of fruit and bread for himself and Mary.

It was tranquil in the stable. As the hours wore on, the music and laughter from the streets faded, and the night became quiet. The stars seemed to brighten as the sky darkened. Joseph lit a candle and its flame flickered goldenly off the straw. The cows and sheep slept on their feet, shaking their heads occasionally. The little donkey stayed awake.

Just after midnight, Mary's baby was born. It was a boy. He cried, but only for a moment. Then he stared around himself with wide, thoughtful eyes. Joseph was overjoyed to be the father of such a fine child, and wanted to show him off to everyone, but no one was there except the animals, so Joseph showed the baby to them. The cows leaned over the rail of their stall and sniffed the child. They breathed sweet air over him, the scent of crops and the sun. The sheep clustered curiously around the baby. They blinked and stared. They wondered why he wasn't coated in wool.

Lastly, Joseph carried the baby to Hazel. The old donkey lowered her face to the infant. His sapphire-blue eyes reflected in her sugar-brown eyes. Her soft white muzzle touched his cheek. "Did you see that, Mary!" Joseph exclaimed. "Our little donkey kissed him."

And Mary smiled, because when a donkey kisses a baby it means the child will share the traits which make the donkey the noblest creature of all: he will be patient, tolerant, modest, forgiving, humorous, gentle and brave. He will be blessed, like the donkey, with peaceful grace. Joseph tickled Hazel between the ears. "Thank you, old girl," he said.

Mary, Joseph, the baby and Hazel rested in the stables for several days. Mary and Joseph wrote their

names for the census, as well as the name of their son. In the meantime, the king had received some appalling news. He'd been told by his wisest advisers that a prince had been born in Bethlehem.

A prince! That would not do. A prince might one day take the crown of a king and boot the king out of the palace, and where would the poor king be then? Out on the streets, with all the horrid people. The king summoned the captain of his soldiers. "Go to Bethlehem," he told the captain. "Kidnap all the boy babies who've been born there in the past two years."

"What shall we do with them then, your Highness?"

"Put them in sacks and bring them to me," replied the king. "And make it snappy."

So the captain took the soldiers and galloped towards Bethlehem.

Meanwhile, in the stables, the old donkey was growing restless. She kicked the walls with her hooves. She whinnied and pawed the straw. "I think she is pining for Ruth," said Mary. "We must take her home, Joseph."

So Joseph packed their possessions, made a sling for the baby, thanked the innkeeper for his hospitality and said goodbye to the sheep and cows. The little group of travellers set out for Nazareth in the cool dawn. Hazel tugged at her rope, hurrying through the sleepy town, and Mary and Joseph had to skip to keep up with her. Mary was tired after all she'd been through and when she'd walked a few miles she needed to rest, but Hazel pulled the rope impatiently, and scuffed the dusty road. She twitched her black tassel of tail and nuzzled Mary with her nose. "Climb on Hazel's back, Mary," Joseph suggested. "Then you can rest from walking, and Hazel needn't stop."

Mary climbed on the donkey's back reluctantly, worried about Hazel's frailty and age. The travellers continued on their journey, Joseph walking beside the donkey, carrying the baby in the sling, the donkey stepping along stoically, picking her way past ridges and rocks. Around midday they saw in the distance a vast legion of the king's soldiers racing towards Bethlehem.

An ashen storm of dust and sand was swirling in its wake. Watching the soldiers fly, Mary and Joseph were glad they had left Bethlehem. It was never good to be in the same place as the king's soldiers.

Hazel tugged the rope. "All right, Hazel!" said Joseph. "We're coming, we're coming."

They walked and walked. Sometimes the baby cried. Flies blew drowsily round the donkey's ears. The sun burned down. The ground was stony, uneven and cracked. Gritty yellow road-dust itched in their eyes. Everything was unpleasant; they were all jaded and sore. The donkey, however, would not stop. She gazed steadfastly towards the horizon, to where Nazareth lay. Each afternoon, when Joseph woke from his nap, the donkey would be standing, alert and waiting, staring into the distance to where the white road disappeared.

After three days of walking, they reached home.

Ruth ran out to meet them. She threw her arms around Hazel's neck. She admired the newborn baby. "Hazel kissed him," said Joseph proudly.

"Ah!" said Ruth, very pleased. "Then he'll bring some good to this world, you'll see."

Joseph, the happy father, took his baby home for a bath. Ruth led Hazel to the shelter and forked out hay for her. She could see that the journey to Bethlehem and back had left her beloved donkey exhausted. She stroked Hazel's cloudy brow; into the long grizzled ears she whispered, "You can rest now."

The next morning, neither Ruth nor Joseph woke to the hee-haw of Hazel. Ruth found the little donkey nestled in the straw, her legs folded neatly beneath her. Her ears drooped towards the ground, she did not lift her head. A small brown sparrow hopped around, fluttering its wings. When it saw Ruth it flew into the rafters, and cheeped fretfully.

Joseph came into the shelter and stood beside Ruth. He gazed sadly down at the donkey. "Oh, Ruth," he said, "I'm sorry."

"Nothing lives forever, Joseph," Ruth replied. "The lucky ones are those who are remembered after they're gone. Be sure to tell your son about Hazel, and your journey to Bethlehem with her. Teach your boy to love animals, to always be kind to them. Hazel would like that, I think."

"I will," Joseph promised, and he kept his word: when his son had grown old enough to understand, Joseph told him of the sheep and cows who'd been first to welcome him into the world, and of the little grey donkey who had rocked him gently, borne him safely, and softly kissed his cheek.

NIGHT UNDER THE TREES

COCO was weeping. "The poor donkey!" she sobbed.

"But the donkey died happy." Marcelle patted her sister's shoulder. "Anyway, it's just a story."

Tears dropped one after another down Coco's face. "Was it just a story?" she implored of the soldier. "Or was it true?"

"You'll have to decide that for yourself, Coco," answered the soldier.

Coco wiped her eyes with the sleeve of her dress. She looked at the silver donkey shining in the soldier's hand. "I will always try to be very good," she sniffed, "just like a donkey."

The soldier smiled. "I can feel night coming," he said. "The air is getting cold. You two must go home now, before somebody comes looking for you."

The girls climbed stiffly to their feet. Marcelle asked the soldier, "Will you be all right, Monsieur, here in the woods by yourself?"

"I will," said the soldier. "I'll be comfortable and warm with these socks and Coco's pillow."

So they bade him good night and promised to return in the morning, and raced each other down the hill to the lane that led them home. At supper that evening, Coco was thoughtful: she had come to the decision that the story of Hazel was definitely true. She asked her mother, "Mama, when I was born, was I kissed by a donkey?"

"No!" Their mother laughed. "What a funny idea, Coco!"

Coco pretended not to see Marcelle's threatening glare. She looked down at her supper, disappointed. She supposed the soldier had been kissed by a donkey when he was a baby. Otherwise he would not be brave enough to sleep in the forest alone.

Beyond the village, in the dark hills, the soldier lay curled at the foot of the tree and listened to the nocturnal sounds of the countryside. The olive army blanket was tucked around him and the silver donkey was where he always carried it, close to his heart. Although he could see only the white fog that palled his eyes, he knew the night must be pitch-black, lightened only by a waxen moon and the occasional shooting star. He heard the wind rummaging through the trees, the fresh leaves tumbling against one another. He heard the calls of night animals – owls, mice, a fox. He was not scared to be in the forest: he knew that trees and creatures and the wind would not hurt him.

But he also knew that he was not brave.

Once, he'd believed he *was* brave, and many other fine things besides. When he'd signed up to become a soldier, he'd been sure he was doing the best thing. Everyone knew the war needed as many soldiers as it could get. His mother and father and sister had been dismayed when he told them what he had done. They'd worried that he would be lost in the war. Nonetheless everybody agreed that signing up *was* the best thing to do. His country needed him, and thousands more young men like him, to defend and preserve it. Anyway, he would not be an ordinary soldier. He came from a wealthy family, he'd gone to the most expensive school, he could speak three languages without making a mistake. He could ride a horse and shoot a pistol and generally be smart as a whip. The army would doubtlessly put him to good use. They wouldn't throw him into the lowly rank-and-file. He'd probably be made a lieutenant, the commander of thirty men. He would tell these men what to do and where to go and how to win the war. He imagined his men would be devoted to him, listen devoutly to his every word. When they went into battle, his soldiers would look to him through the smoke and chaos and, seeing him fighting like a lion, would fight like lions themselves.

Curled up shivering in the forest, the soldier chuckled to himself. How foolish he'd been, in those early days! He'd been silly and proud as a rooster.

The army did make him a lieutenant. They did put him in charge of thirty men. These men were young and tough and poor. At home they'd been coalminers, boilermakers, street-sweepers, ice-men. They thought that he, their Lieutenant, was scrawny and ridiculous. Sometimes he heard them laughing after he'd walked by. Nevertheless he strove to treat the men well. He tried to be fair, understanding and good-humoured. And, because he was all these things, his men came to admire him, as he admired them. They bragged to other soldiers about what a decent chap their

Lieutenant was. They stopped laughing when he walked past; instead they invited him to join their card games and had him check their letters for spelling errors. And he had done his best, month after month, to keep them all fed and healthy and alive.

Of course, in war it is impossible to keep every soldier alive. For every man that was lost, the soldier grieved as if for a brother. He spent wretched nights in filthy trenches writing to faraway mothers and fathers, telling them their son was gone. He watched as his men became dispirited, cynical, cold-blooded, ill. And he hated the war, and could never shake from his mind the memory of the dreadful things he'd seen.

It was cold and lonesome in the beech and elm forest, but on the breeze the soldier could hear the muffled sound of rolling waves – the Channel. The Channel was thirty-five kilometres of freezing green water, but thirty-five kilometres seemed a short distance, compared to how far he'd already come. Much better to be here, alone and chilled but feeling close to home, than back there in the unspeakable trenches.

But at least, back there, they had called him a brave man: here, hiding amid the leaves and shadows, they would call him a coward.

A NEWCOMER IN THE WOODS

I N the morning, it was raining. "Our poor soldier!" cried Marcelle, as she speedily dressed against the weather. "He'll be soaked to the skin!"

"Our beautiful soldier will be drowned!" wailed Coco.

"We must go to him as fast as we can," declared Marcelle, pulling on her boots.

The sisters ran downstairs. "Mama!" said Marcelle. "May we go out and pick mushrooms for Juliette?" Juliette was the family pig.

Their mother was sitting on a stool at the stove, toasting bread on a fork. The toast filled the house with a mouth-watering aroma. "Haven't you noticed it's raining?" she said. "You'll stay inside and keep dry for school. Save your breakfast crusts for Juliette, and there'll be milk left over for her."

Marcelle and Coco jigged with frustration. "But we must go out, Mama!" Coco whined. "It's important! We'll take Papa's umbrella – can we, Papa?"

Their father was home from the dairy for breakfast. He hugged a mug of warm milk in chilly hands. "What's so important that my Coco must go out in the rain and become a drowned rat?" he asked.

Coco thought quickly. She couldn't mention the soldier – she had promised that. "There's a family of elves in the woods," she answered inventively. "They said we must visit them this morning, before school."

"Yes!" said Marcelle, impressed with her sister's fib. "They're going to teach us elf magic!"

Pascal was sitting close to the stove, a slice of toast balanced on his knees. "Elves in the forest!" he scoffed. "Trolls, more like it."

Coco frowned. "No, not trolls – elves!"

"I've heard there's trolls in the woods – hundreds of them. With big teeth and bad breath."

"These are elves," Coco insisted. "They're small and dressed in blue."

"They could be trolls in disguise. Trolls like wearing blue."

Coco felt wild. "Trolls only live under bridges, Pascal! Elves live in the forest!"

"No, that's not true." Pascal crunched his toast. "Trolls live everywhere. And they often disguise themselves as magical elves, just to trick silly girls."

"Mama! Pascal's being horrible! You're so horrible, Pascal!"

"Shush now, all of you," said the children's mother. "Marcelle, here's your breakfast. Remember to save the crusts for Juliette. Coco, where is your satchel? You'll be late for school if you've lost it. Madame Hugo will be stopping me in the street again, telling the whole village I don't care about your education. My face went bright red."

"She is very scary, that Madame Hugo," agreed the children's father.

The sisters looked at each other helplessly. There was nothing they could do. They would have to leave the soldier alone and hungry in the rain.

It was an awful day for Marcelle. She could not stop thinking about the poor soldier. She thought about the silver donkey and old, heroic Hazel. She thought about the soldier's brother, John, lying sickly in a white room on the far side of the sea. She imagined his cries as he writhed feverishly at night. *Lieutenant!* he would call pathetically. *Lieutenant, where are you?*

And Lieutenant couldn't answer him because he

was sitting in the woods in the rain on the other side of the Channel, and the only people who knew he was there were two young girls, one of whom – Coco – was standing on a box at the front of the room and reciting the nine-times table. Marcelle listened with one ear. Coco was clever, and didn't stumble over the sums, not even when she reached nine-times-eight, which Marcelle always thought was hard. "Nine-times-eight is seventy-two," sang Coco like a blackbird. Marcelle sighed, and stared bleakly out the window. The rain was falling and falling. The glass in the window was foggy with cold. Coco was smart, but not smart enough to think of a way to help the soldier go home. And Marcelle, who had racked her brains, couldn't think of a way either.

They needed the help of somebody smarter. But they'd promised not to tell anyone about the soldier, so how could they ask for somebody's help? It was a predicament.

When the rain eased off after lunch Madame Hugo

rang the bell and released the children, who flew on high spirits through the wet streets, splashing the puddles. Coco and Marcelle tore home, where Coco kept her mother occupied with questions while Marcelle raided the kitchen for food. The soldier would be ravenous, and frozen to the core. She stuffed her satchel with a loaf of bread, a slice of cheese, a cup of sugar, a jar of dried apple: the pantry shelf now looked bare. To make amends for not visiting him that morning, she decided to give the soldier a gift. From her father's dressing-table drawer she took Papa's second-best shaving razor. His best razor was nicer, but Papa would soon notice it was gone.

She waved to Coco from the doorway. "We will finish our discussion later, Mama," said Coco, and raced from the room before her mother could say a word.

The sisters walked side-by-side down the lane.

Marcelle carried the satchel over her shoulder. It bulged with the shape of a loaf of bread. Coco gazed at the tumultuous sky. "The poor soldier," she groaned.

"I hope he's not dead," murmured Marcelle.

"Dead! Could he be dead? Why would he be dead?"

"He might have caught pneumonia and faded away."

"Oh! I will cry if that's happened!" promised Coco. They both reflected on the fact that, just yesterday, they'd found the soldier in the woods and thought him dead then, too. Now that they were fond of him, the soldier's demise seemed much more poignant, and much more likely. "I wonder if he'd let me keep the silver donkey," mused Coco. "If he's dead, I mean."

Unexpectedly a figure rounded the corner of the stone-walled lane. The girls were close enough to see that the figure was their brother Pascal. He had loitered with his friends in the village after school. Now he was coming home with sodden shoes and a fish hooked on his fingers. "Look," he said, brandishing the fish. "Fabrice gave it to me for dinner."

Fabrice was Pascal's friend who owned the motorcycle. He worked at the harbour, repairing the nets and boats. Sometimes he would dangle a line off the pier to catch whatever was swimming by. The seaweedy smell of the fish made Marcelle and Coco screw up their faces.

"Revolting!" scolded Marcelle.

"Not revolting, *très bon!* Where are you going? On another picnic, in this weather?"

"It's none of your business!" hissed Coco.

Pascal looked amused. "Are you going to visit the elves who wear blue?"

"It's not your business, Pascal! Leave us alone!"

"Ah-ha! So you are going to visit the elves! Can I come?"

"You don't even believe in elves," Coco scowled.

"But that's why I want to meet *your* elves," replied Pascal reasonably.

Marcelle was eyeing the glassy-eyed fish. "If you come with us," she said suddenly, "you must swear to keep everything you see a secret."

Coco spun to her, horrified. "Marcelle!"

"You must swear on your life, Pascal. It is important."

"Marcelle!" yelped Coco. "Don't!"

Pascal shrugged and smiled carelessly. "I swear upon my life."

"Also," said Marcelle, "you must donate your fish."

Pascal glanced at the fish. "Elves eat fish," said Marcelle.

Coco was tugging her sister's sleeve. "Marcie," she whimpered, "you promised not to tell. *You promised!*"

Marcelle didn't answer. She started walking, and Pascal and Coco followed. She hoped that, when she explained things to the soldier, he would understand why she had brought Pascal to the forest. She didn't think it mattered if Coco understood or not.

They climbed the hills and were dampened by rain which beaded on the grass and pooled in secret puddles that the grass hid from view. The hills were dotted with wildflowers, their petals bruised by raindrops. Coco trudged in silence behind her brother and sister, pouting unhappily. She hoped the soldier would be angry with Marcelle. She hoped that Pascal would tell the whole village about the soldier and then everyone would be angry at Marcelle.

As they drew nearer to the soldier's nook, Marcelle told Pascal, "Stay here."

Pascal stopped beneath a birch tree, the fish dangling at his knees. Above and all around him, the ghostly branches dripped. Marcelle crept onward, into the woods; Coco followed, chewing her lip. As furious as she was, she had not forgotten that the soldier was possibly dead from pneumonia.

But he was sitting up against the tree, his blanket draped over his head. His hands were gloved in Papa's socks and tucked into his armpits. He peeked past the blanket's hem when he heard footsteps approach. Sometimes he forgot that he couldn't see.

"Marcelle?" he said uneasily. "Coco?"

"It's us," said Marcelle.

The soldier was relieved. "I thought you had forgotten me!"

"We hadn't, Monsieur Lieutenant. Mama wouldn't let us go out this morning, because of all the rain."

"We've been so worried about you!" Coco told him, agonized. "We thought you might have washed away, or caught your death from cold."

"The rain doesn't bother me," the soldier assured them. He'd been soaked to the skin many times in the war. He'd spent months sloshing through quaggy trenches. "I'm used to it."

Coco could contain herself no longer. "Our brother Pascal is hiding in the trees, Lieutenant. Marcelle brought him here – not me!"

"I had to bring him, Lieutenant," said Marcelle. To Coco's confusion, her sister sounded sad. "I can't think of a way for you to get home. Coco can't think of one, either. But Pascal is clever, and he's thirteen. He might be able to think of a plan, and you can go home to your mama and papa and John."

The soldier gazed blindly at Marcelle. She could not look at him. Then the soldier said loudly, "Pascal? Where are you?"

"I'm here," said Pascal, stepping from the shadows. He had not waited under the birch tree for more than a minute before trailing his sisters into the woods. He'd been very curious to see the elves they were talking about. He did not believe elves existed. He'd been surprised to see the blanket-draped man sitting cross-legged under the trees, but he would have been much more surprised to see elves. "*Bonjour*, Monsieur," he said politely.

"His name is Monsieur Lieutenant Shepard," Coco told her brother. "Monsieur is blind. You can't tell anyone that he's here. You promised you wouldn't, remember!"

Pascal had noticed in an instant the man's army-issue boots. He knew that *Lieutenant* wasn't a real name, but a rank of officer in the army. Pascal guessed immediately that a lieutenant hiding in a forest was someone who'd run away from the war. Soldiers who ran away from the war could be severely punished. They could be thrown in prison, or shot. Pascal was rather pleased to make the acquaintance of someone who might be shot. He could understand why the soldier needed to be kept a secret.

"It's nice to meet you, Pascal," said the soldier.

"And you, Lieutenant," the boy replied. "How did you lose your sight? Were you hit by shrapnel? Were your eyes burned by poison gas?"

The soldier answered, "It's a long story, I'm afraid."

"We brought some food, Monsieur," interrupted Marcelle. She took the bread, sugar, apples and cheese from her school bag. "Pascal's brought a fish, too. We can light a fire and cook it for your supper."

"We can't light a fire," said Pascal. "There's no dry fire-wood anywhere around."

Marcelle saw this was true, and felt foolish, but at

least the soldier had heard for himself how intelligent Pascal could be. She said, "Monsieur Shepard needs your help, Pascal."

"Mine?" Pascal was flattered. "How?"

"He must go home to see his brother, who is ill and calls out at night. But first he must cross the sea, and at its narrowest place the Channel is thirty-five kilometres wide."

"And that's too far to swim," added Coco. "Also, he is blind. He might swim in a circle and end up back where he started."

In one quick moment, Pascal thought of an idea. He didn't mention it to his sisters and the soldier – he first wanted to think the plan through in private. Meanwhile Coco asked the soldier, "May I see the silver donkey?"

The soldier took the silver donkey from his pocket. Coco showed the little object to Pascal. "This is Monsieur Lieutenant's lucky charm. Isn't it lovely? It kept him safe in the war – it *still* keeps him safe, even though he's blind! Will you tell us another story, Monsieur?"

Pascal was not interested in a silver donkey, but he was very interested in hearing gruesome stories about the war. He sat down on a rock, rubbing his cold hands. Coco sat beside him, her arms wrapped round her knees. Marcelle used her father's razor to slice the bread and cheese, and while the soldier told his story the four of them shared a genteel afternoon tea beneath the dripping trees.

THE SECOND TALE

ONCE long ago, a fearful thing happened in the world: the great monsoon, which had faithfully brought life-giving rain for as long as the plants and people and animals could remember, inexplicably failed to arrive. The sky had looked down on the world and seen many things that displeased it: vexed and disappointed it had decided, "I will not rain."

On Earth, the dry season had been long. It had left

the ground baked stony and the trees bare of leaves. The rivers had shrunk into muddy pools. The grass had withered and blown away. Everyone and everything was waiting impatiently for the monsoon. Its rain would return life to a world that was parched as an Egyptian mummy. It would give colour to all that had been scorched brown. To the people, the plants and animals who had struggled through the hard months of the dry, the monsoon would bring mercy. All living things watched the sky for sight of the first storm cloud. "The rain will come soon," they promised each other.

But the rain did not come.

Days went by; then weeks. The sky should have been turbulent with storms. Spears of lightning should have flared from the clouds. The grass should have been springing up fresh and green from the cracked orange ground. The riverbanks should have washed away under the mighty force of driving rain. But none of this was happening. The sky stayed dazzlingly, painfully, blue, and the sun continued to blaze.

There was no rain – not a drop.

At first, the people were puzzled. Never in living memory had they known the monsoon to fail. They were confident that, shortly, the rain would arrive. "The monsoon is like a beloved friend who's fallen asleep on a hot afternoon," they told one another. "Any moment now, it will wake up and remember that we're expecting it here, and that it's running impolitely late."

The people agreed that they could forgive their beloved friend this tardiness, as long as it arrived soon – before everyone got very hungry, before what scant water remained evaporated into the heavens.

But the sky stayed blue.

A month passed. The sky stayed blue. The scent of saffron, which for centuries had sweetened the air, faded, and was replaced by the odour of dust.

Trees which had survived the dry seasons of a hundred years could not endure this new, ferocious, unending dry: they began to creak and moan in their sleep, and crashed to their knees like hurt beasts.

Animals stood where lakes
had once been, and
did not move.

Babies were
born, and the sun
beat on them, and
they cried for a drop
of moisture, and
struggled against
the misery of this forsaken world.

The people stared furiously up at the sky. "Rain!"
they commanded it. "How dare you ignore us! *Rain*,
you slothful sky!"

But the sky stared blandly back at them. It would
not be bullied. In fact, one of the things it liked least
about people was their tendency to bully. So the sky
merely stared, as if not understanding a word, and
continued to shine down a burning-hot face.

Soon there was almost no water left. Buckets
dropped into wells brought up only handfuls of stones.

The pools which had been rivers became puddles which had been pools. The fish had no home now. The soil was becoming sand. Pastureland, which should have been sprouting crops that stood strong and tall, instead was swathes of stark red dust. And for the people and plants and animals, there was nothing to drink.

When there is nothing to drink and nothing to eat, there is famine. A weakness and a weariness spreads throughout the land. The living things lie down because they have no strength
to stand.

The people and animals of the barren country were not angry now. Anger was too exhausting. They were simply dejected and defeated. "The sky doesn't care about us," the people muttered. The bones of every living thing showed cruelly through its skin.

Not all the people, however, were willing to accept a waterless fate. One morning a small crowd gathered in the thorny shade of a jujube tree. The crowd had decided it was time they gave the sky a good talking-to. The sky had to see the error of its ways. It had no right thinking it could do what it wanted, when it wanted. To take their indignation to the sky, the people climbed the highest mountain. It was hard and thirsty work, climbing the mountain. The sun blazed down; the dust floated up. The people were quite dizzy and enfeebled when they arrived at the peak. Nonetheless they shouted with gusto at the blue, blue sky. "What game do you think you're playing, sky?" they bawled. "Look at the world – what do you see? An ever-growing desert! We want the monsoon: it is our right to have it. It is your task to provide it. So do what you are supposed to do, and *rain!*"

The sky hung over the fuming people. "I will not," it replied.

"*What?*" screamed the people. "Why *not?*"

"Because you did not say *please*," said the sky.

The people danced and shrieked with rage. "We don't need to say please to the sky! It is your job to make us happy! Otherwise, what is the use of you?"

"I am more use to *you* than you are to *me*," answered the sky darkly. "Go away, you who think the entire world is yours to command."

The people danced in rage some more, and then cried and pleaded piteously, and promised to be well-behaved, but the sky was not persuaded. It had seen people break promises before. Eventually there was nothing for the people to do but stagger back down the mountainside. Some of them were weeping. Others had a plan. "If the selfish sky won't listen to the people, perhaps it will listen to the animals. They, too, are thirsty."

So the people sought out the most impressive creature they knew of: the mighty elephant. They told the elephant what it must do. The elephant approved. It laboured slowly up the mountain and stood swaying at the peak. It raised its trunk and trumpeted for the sky's attention. "Sky!" it bellowed. "See how big I am! I could crush you with a single foot! Why don't you rain, you lazy thing? Are you afraid of hard work? I am not afraid of hard work. I am strong and tremendous! I can knock down houses and trees. I could trample this mountain into rubble. If you don't bring the monsoon now, I will use my trunk to squeeze the water out of you!"

"Elephant," said the sky, "you are strong, it's true. You are magnificent, so the people worship you. But, like them, you are arrogant. Like them, you use your power the wrong way. You can try to squeeze rain out of me, but I don't think you'll succeed."

The elephant, gravely insulted, tried to wrap its trunk round the sky and give it a dreadful squeezing. But although the elephant could see the sky, it somehow couldn't touch it. The sky was only made of air, and even an elephant's incredible strength cannot squeeze a monsoon out of air. The elephant tried its best all day and night, because it did not like to fail any task put before it. Eventually, though, it recognized defeat, and shambled in shame down the mountain.

A handsome tiger, who had heard about the attempt to make the sky rain, was waiting at the foot of the mountain. It watched the vanquished elephant collapse in a heap in the dirt. It showed its invincible teeth in disgust. "If you want a job done properly, ask a cat to do it," the tiger said, and bounded up the mountainside.

The air was muggy at the peak. "Sky," purred the tiger, "it's me, admirable me. Where's the rain, sky? Not only does tiger want a drink, but there's no pools to reflect tiger's pretty face. The whole world fears me, sky, and so they should. Tiger is beautiful, but also fearsome. Tiger's terrible with tooth and claw. If you don't make quick with the monsoon, sky, I'll show you how terrible tiger can be."

The sky blew a breeze that ruffled the tiger's whiskers. "It's true you are beautiful, tiger," it said. "It's a pity you are sneaky and a coward. You only use your teeth and claws on those weaker than yourself – against creatures that cannot fight back. And you always attack from behind."

The tiger yelled with fury, humiliated to the core. It sprang at the sky, teeth and claws bared. But the sky is an uncatchable thing: claws cannot scar it, and teeth cannot hold it. The tiger leapt a hundred times at the sky, but the sky was unmarked and unmoved. It was a very sorry cat that dragged itself limping down the mountainside.

At the foot of the mountain a glittering snake was coiled. It watched with soulless, unblinking eyes as the tiger slunk away. It kept its opinion to itself, as snakes always do. Calmly it wove between the boulders that dotted the mountainside. It was in no hurry to reach the peak. It was confident that, once it hissed a quiet word in the sky's ear, the world would find itself awash with rain. There might possibly be a minor flood before the snake even slithered off the mountain. "Sky," it whispered, from the windless peak, "it is I. Your friend, snake."

The sky gave a gusty laugh. "Snake," it said, "you're a teller of untruths. You are a friend to none but yourself. You have only your own interests in your cold heart. Go away, little serpent, and hide under a rock."

The snake, unlike the elephant and tiger, knew better than to waste energy arguing. It did not attempt to bite the sky. That would be pointless, and a waste of venom. It slid down the mountain, seething sound lessly, and pulled its black hood over its face as it passed the crowd around the jujube tree.

Amid the crowd was a newcomer. A young yellow dog, bursting with enthusiasm, couldn't wait to address the sky. It galloped up the mountain, its tongue flying like a banner. "Sky!" it woofed. "Please look at me! Please pay attention to me! Look down at all the poor people, sky! Why don't you love them as much as I do? I love them, oh I love them. If I was the sky, and the people wanted rain, I would rain! I would do it, just to please them! What's the matter with you, sky? You're not loyal. You're not well-trained. You're rather disobedient. You've probably got fleas!"

"Dog," sighed the sky, "you know that I adore you, for you can be so adorable. But you are not without fault. You are devoted to the point of stupidity. You haven't a mind of your own."

"What's a mind-of-your-own?" asked the dog. "Can I eat it? Can I bury it? Can I chase it down the road?"

"Go away, pup," said the sky tiredly. "Run back to your masters. Tell them I will not discuss the monsoon any more. All this chatter is simply making me annoyed. I have seen and heard nothing that proves you deserve what you demand."

The dog barked non-stop at the sky for several hours, but the sky did not change its mind, so finally the dog loped down the mountain and repeated the sky's message to its masters. "Oh dear," murmured the people, "we are doomed."

All day a donkey had been standing in a scrap of shade. Now it stepped cautiously into the sunlight. The people and animals looked sharply at it. "Where do you think you're going?" they snapped. "Don't you dare go up that mountain! Things are bad enough without you making us look silly! We may be hungry and thirsty, but we haven't lost so much dignity that a moth-eaten donkey must plead on our behalf!"

So the donkey retreated, and stood in silence while the day wore out and night drew down, and the temperature cooled a little, and the crowd of people and animals fell asleep; then the donkey left its place under the jujube and walked up the mountainside.

The night was starry. The sky had turned panther-blue. There were no clouds to blot the brightness of the moon. The donkey looked down from the mountain's peak and saw the sweltering world spread out below its hooves.

It saw great dunes and palm trees, sandy bowls where lakes had been. It saw abandoned houses and bony herds of cows.

"Donkey." The sky spoke suddenly, cold anger in its voice. "Why have you come here? I told the dog that none were to approach me."

The donkey hung its head and trembled, but it did not flee. The sky flamed black and purple with agitation. It said, "Have you been sent to threaten me, as the others were? You are wasting your time. I am not frightened of you, donkey. You may kick and bray till your long ears chime, but you won't make any difference."

The donkey did not answer, but glanced meekly at the sky. The sky understood, then, that the people and the animals hadn't sent the donkey to the peak. The sky knew that the people and other animals scorned donkeys. They thought of donkeys as stubborn and thick-headed brutes, and were surely too proud to let such a creature speak on their behalf. The sky churned, growing reflective. Its colour deepened to jaguar-black. It said, "You have come here, donkey, and risked my wrath, to plead for rain. Yet the monsoon will only benefit those who treat you badly. Donkeys are despised as witless and pig-headed. You are forced to carry impossible loads, whipped till your hides are crossed with scars. You are fed the harshest food, and very little of it. When you are too worn to work, you are cast aside. Yours can be a thankless life, donkey. So often you are treated not as a feeling creature, but as an insensible lump of clay. Wouldn't it be better, donkey, if this unkind world shrivelled and simply blew away?"

The donkey looked into the stars. It raised its voice bravely and said, "It's true that I have known suffering, sky. That's why I cannot bear the sight of it."

The sky was surprised. "Those who have treated you without pity, donkey, are now tasting pitilessness for themselves. This should make you happy."

The donkey shook its tousled head. "It does not make me happy, sky. I will not take pleasure in the suffering of others. I would rather endure suffering myself, than see it inflicted on the world in my name."

The sky was touched by the donkey's words. It swirled around the animal's hooves, flurrying the dirt into dust-devils. Quietly it said, "Often I have looked down on the world and despaired. I have seen the deplorable things that people do to each other. I did not bring the monsoon because I thought there were none who deserved a beautiful home. All hearts were barren, I believed, and deserved only a barren world. But your heart isn't like that, donkey. You endure much that is unforgivable, yet you forgive. And if you, a simple donkey, can have mercy, then surely I, the boundless sky, can be merciful also. Come closer, little donkey, let me see you."

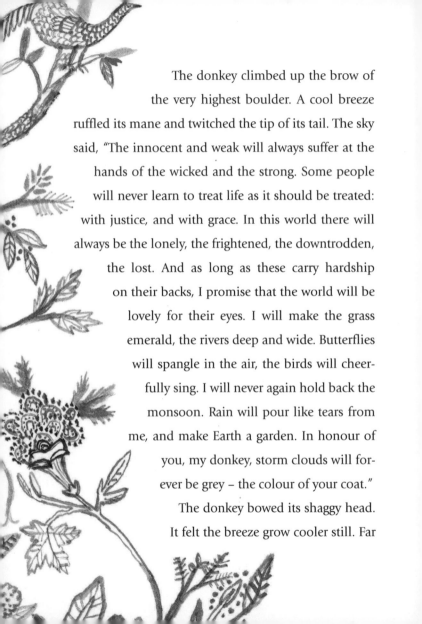

The donkey climbed up the brow of
the very highest boulder. A cool breeze
ruffled its mane and twitched the tip of its tail. The sky
said, "The innocent and weak will always suffer at the
hands of the wicked and the strong. Some people
will never learn to treat life as it should be treated:
with justice, and with grace. In this world there will
always be the lonely, the frightened, the downtrodden,
the lost. And as long as these carry hardship
on their backs, I promise that the world will be
lovely for their eyes. I will make the grass
emerald, the rivers deep and wide. Butterflies
will spangle in the air, the birds will cheer-
fully sing. I will never again hold back the
monsoon. Rain will pour like tears from
me, and make Earth a garden. In honour of
you, my donkey, storm clouds will forever be grey – the colour of your coat."

The donkey bowed its shaggy head.
It felt the breeze grow cooler still. Far

away on the horizon, a pearly streak of lightning flashed. "Hurry away, little donkey," breathed the twisting sky. "I think it will soon rain. When it falls, know that it is falling not for those who demand everything, but for those who ask so little."

So the donkey turned and made its way down the mountain as the first small raindrops hit the parched ground. The drops grew rapidly larger and larger until they were big as pebbles. The dirt was stained black in a moment, and minuscule rivers ran between the stones. Water soaked the donkey's dusty coat and brought relief to the animal's tired bones. Soon the rain was driving down, urgent as a waterfall. From overflowing cracks in the earth rose the scent of nutmeg and vanilla. In days to follow, fresh leaves would decorate the trees, and flowers would dot the new-greened land.

Around the prickly jujube tree, the people and animals danced. They washed themselves in the pelting rain and opened their mouths to catch the drops. They sang and shouted and applauded one another. They believed that they had beaten the sky, that they had bullied it into bringing the monsoon. They did not notice the donkey who walked among them, returning to its place by the tree. It stopped under the streaming branches and seemed never to have gone. Amid the noisy, exultant crowd, beneath the stormy, foaming sky, drenched by roaring, torrential rain, the donkey stood, a speck of silence, serene.

THE IDEAS MAN

PASCAL tried to be polite, but he was quite disappointed with that story. He had hoped the soldier would tell them riveting adventures from the war, not stories about donkeys who had conversations with the sky. He would have preferred a tale about machine-guns and bayonets. Even Coco was not happy. "It's not fair!" she complained. "The poor donkey! Why does the donkey have to suffer?"

"It's just a story," said Pascal to console her, but she shot him a deadly glance.

"The donkey saved everyone, Coco," said Marcelle. "Would you like it better if the whole world had dried up and blown away?"

"Yes, I would!" Coco said fiercely. "I *would* like that better!"

Pascal laughed at her. "You're just being silly, Thérèse," he said. "Don't you think so, Lieutenant?"

"Coco is never silly," answered the soldier.

Pascal decided it was high time the subject of donkeys was dropped. He said, "Tell me about the war, Lieutenant. Have you been fighting at the Front?"

The soldier ate the last of the cheese. "Yes, I have."

Pascal leaned forward on the rock. "What did you see there? What did you do? Have you fired a machine-gun? Did you shoot anyone? Have you been to the desert? Have you sailed on a warship? Do you have any medals? Have you thrown a grenade?"

"Pascal," said Marcelle, "don't ask him those things!"

Pascal ignored his sister. "Is it true what they say, Lieutenant – that the enemy is going to win the war?"

The soldier knew he should reassure the boy that the enemy certainly would not win. Instead he said honestly, "I don't know, Pascal. I only know that the fighting is dreadful."

"Tell me about it!" Pascal caught his breath. "No one in the village knows anything! Madame Hugo, our teacher, pretends the war isn't happening! She says that children shouldn't think of such things. But I want to know everything about it."

"Pascal, be quiet!" protested Marcelle. "You're upsetting Monsieur Lieutenant, asking him these questions!

He doesn't want to talk about the war! The war is awful, like Papa says. Don't remind Monsieur of it!"

"I knew this would happen!" cried Coco bitterly. "Everything is spoiled now! This place was nice – it was *our* place, Marcelle! – and now all we can talk about is stupid guns! It's *your* fault, Marcie – I told you not to bring Pascal here!"

The brother and sisters glared at each other. The soldier licked the taste of cheese from his thumbs. He said, "Thank you for the picnic, Marcelle. It was kind of you to bring it. I cannot imagine what would have happened, had you and Coco not found me."

Marcelle beamed. "I'm sorry there wasn't much food, Monsieur. We'll bring something else tomorrow."

"Yes." Pascal stood up, brushing dirt from the fish. "Evening's coming – we should go home. We'll come again tomorrow, as soon as we can."

"Marcie just told him we would!" shouted Coco.

Her brother continued unperturbed. "I wish we

could hide you in a barn or cellar, Lieutenant. Some-where you'd be out of the weather. But somebody might find you, and that would mean trouble. Tomorrow, when we come, I will whistle – like this." Pascal pursed his lips and gave a tuneful whistle. "It will be our secret password. That way, when you hear it, you'll know it's only us. If you hear other footsteps but don't hear the whistle, you must stay still and try to be invisible."

Marcelle was cross that she hadn't thought of a secret password whistle, but she was also proud of Pascal for being bright enough to invent it. Coco, too, was charmed by the idea – having a secret password made everything mysterious and daring. She tried out the whistle for herself. "That was a good try, Coco," said Pascal, "but it wasn't quite right. Only I can do it properly. Tomorrow, when we come here, you'd better let me do the whistling. Otherwise the Lieutenant will get confused."

"All right," said Coco grudgingly.

Marcelle wrung her hands. "I wish you were warm, Monsieur. I wish your boots and blanket were dry. I wish it hadn't rained."

"Lieutenant Shepard is a soldier," answered her brother. "A soldier is strong. A soldier isn't bothered by wet boots. Anyway, this will soon be over. I think I know how to help the Lieutenant go home."

"Oh no!" squeaked Coco.

"How?" gasped Marcelle.

Pascal looked superior. "I'll tell you my plan tomorrow, or maybe the next day. I need to work out the details. I might have to tell someone else you are here. Just one other person – all right, Lieutenant?"

The soldier nodded, though he felt his heart sink. In Pascal's words he heard his bid for freedom crumble apart. *One other person* would tell yet one *more* person, who'd tell another and another and another. Soon there would be a great crowd gathered in the forest, staring down at the soldier as if he were a peculiar and unpleasant bug. Soon somebody would realize that the soldier's eyes weren't actually blind but simply tired of seeing, and stubbornly refusing to see. Soon someone would decide that a man who was clearly not a bug should, in fact, be fighting at the Front. "Whatever you think is best, Pascal," said the soldier quietly.

"Good night then, Lieutenant," Pascal said, and saluted the soldier smartly, although the soldier couldn't see.

"Here is the silver donkey, Monsieur."

The soldier felt small fingers brush his own, and then the warmed weight of the lucky charm that Coco placed on his palm.

THE FRONT

ALONE in the silent woods at night, it was easy for the soldier to remember the war. Inside the fog that clouded his eyes, he saw the colours of war; beyond the silence of the night, he heard the battle cries.

The soldier could have told Pascal some stories about the war.

As soon as he'd been put in command, the soldier had learned the names of the thirty men he commanded – he thought every officer should do this. As well as this, he tried to remember certain things that made each man different from his fellows. Tommy Drake bred goldfish; Joe Webster carved furniture from wood. Eddy Hobbs had a gift for drawing; Arthur Harris could play the flute. A swinging gate had snipped off the tip of Will Palmer's left thumb. Such things could be difficult to remember, but the Lieutenant made himself do it. He didn't think it was right to send a man into battle without caring to know anything about that man.

The trenches in which he and his platoon had lived were deep and narrow and dirty, fanning out across the fields like an odious spider's web. It was easy to get lost in the grim network of passages. The trenches stank of wet earth and decay, reminding the soldiers of a graveyard. Sometimes the trenches would cave in, and then everyone would dig as fast as they could to rescue the men who'd been buried.

The enemy had their own trenches. The noise of gun-fire and shelling went on almost ceaselessly, but in rare moments of quiet the enemy could be heard talking and laughing and worrying with one another. The enemy soldiers sounded young – some of them had the fresh voices of boys. The Lieutenant supposed that some of them played the flute or carved wood or could draw; and that all of them had mothers and fathers waiting and wondering at home.

Here and there, throughout the trenches, troughs the length and depth of a man had been gouged from the claggy walls. The troughs were for sleeping in, though it was nearly impossible to sleep. There was too much noise, and too much tension. Lieutenant Shepard, when he dozed, dreamed of waking to find the trenches deserted, his comrades having abandoned him to fight the enemy alone.

Sometimes a week would go by before the men could rest and take off their boots. Everyone would hold their noses. They would laugh at themselves, at how uncivilized they'd become. Then their laughter would fade at the sight of their feet, the ankles and toes rubbed raw.

They were always hungry and thirsty. The army gave them bully-beef and biscuits to eat. The biscuits were so hard that they chipped the soldiers' teeth. Rain filled bowls scooped from the mud and the soldiers dipped their fingers in it.

On the greatest and most wonderful days, the mail would arrive. The luckiest received parcels, inside which were books, handkerchiefs, almonds, soap, and lovely clean knitted socks. The mail brought other precious things: letters from home. The soldier who got nothing in the mail would struggle not to weep. The other men were sorry for him.

The men had been strangers at the beginning of the war. But as the months went by and they lived shoulder-to-shoulder in the trenches, sharing jokes and memories and dreaming of life after the war, the men became friends. They came to trust and care for each other. As time went on, they became brothers. They knew they would fight and even die to protect one another. And it seemed, to the Lieutenant, miraculous, that a thing as terrible as the war could forge between strangers such unbreakable bonds.

And fight they did; and die.

Sometimes Lieutenant Shepard thought that the war was not a battle between men but between mighty unseen gods or devils who used the men as ammunition. These gods or devils were not mindful: rather, they were like spoiled children playing roughly with toys, seeing no reason to be careful, knowing that what was broken or lost would be magically replaced. It didn't matter to them that the men were scarcely more than boys, that they had mothers and fathers, siblings and friends, hopes and wishes, sweethearts and pets. The orders came and the soldiers had to go – out into no-man's-land with their rifles at their hips. In the trenches they would leave behind letters addressed to home. These letters read, *Take care, dearest, we'll meet again some day.*

But it wasn't gods and devils who were responsible for the war – it was ordinary men. The ordinary men issued commands and the soldiers bravely obeyed, plunging across the quagmired earth in a fraught attempt to claw from the enemy a handful of ground. In the stinking expanse of no-man's-land, only the colour of their uniforms stood between a soldier and his enemy.

But men fell in other places, too. A soldier could go to visit the chaplain, to bandage an injury, to pass on a joke. And, if he found himself in the wrong place, he wouldn't return. Massive shells roared from the sky. Shrapnel sprayed like razors. Snipers popped up quick as jack-rabbits. So the Lieutenant's thirty men gradually became fewer, and the ones who survived became flinty-eyed believers in fate. Each bullet that whistled harmlessly by made them tougher, smarter, faster. Their Lieutenant was amazed by how courageous they were. The Lieutenant himself thought that each harmless bullet simply brought him closer to the bullet that would do great harm.

Lieutenant Shepard's men were tough, smart, fast

and brave, too good to waste: but wasted they were, as the Lieutenant knew they would be, for war is only waste.

His platoon, and many others, received orders to leave the trenches and walk out into no-man's-land. Somewhere, someone must have had a grand plan: the Lieutenant was told only a bit of it. He and his men would be among the faceless many who would creep like rats in a wide half-circle and surprise the enemy from behind. It seemed a fragile, foolhardy idea. In the hours before the attack began, the men were subdued. They wrote letters to their wives and families. They tried to think of fitting words. They weren't used to putting their feelings on paper. They read their letters to the Lieutenant. *How does that sound to you, sir?*

The Lieutenant wrote his own letter. *Dearest Mother, it seems we are about to embark …*

In the misty drifting light of dawn the signal was given and Lieutenant Shepard's platoon took its place behind others and set off. They kept to the dark gullies and swampy lower ground. They carried their rifles across their chests. The earth was slippery and slick. Men gripped one another's arms to keep from falling down. As they passed a stand of crooked trees a raven took to the air. The Lieutenant watched it flap away. He could not remember the last time he had seen a bird. He thought suddenly of the robins which scratched the soil below the dining-room window at home.

The mist lay thick; the men kept close. Nobody spoke. The sky was grainy, smoky and sour. It was impossible to see more than a few paces ahead. Broken black trees twisted up from the mud. The Lieutenant's face was damp. The men stepped silently, like foxes in a forest.

They came upon the enemy unexpectedly. No one was prepared. A cry of surprise went up from both sides. A burst of ruby, flame-thrown light flashed against the sky. The Lieutenant saw the shadows of men toppling. For a moment, everything was helter-skelter. The officers screamed for order. The earth erupted

as shells crashed down, dirt flung through the air like seaspray. The Lieutenant thought of foamy waves hitting a rocky shore at the tatty torn edge of the world.

He was where he should be, at the head of his platoon. Shells exploded suddenly in a fiery circle around him. His legs buckled with the shock, his chin struck the ground. He dropped into a shallow pocket in the muck and stayed there. It was as protected as any place could be. The sky flared amber and turquoise. He looked around desperately for his men and saw them lying like dolls in the mud, their limbs bent every which way. Some of them gasped and mutely writhed; most of them lay still. The gods and devils had run their claws through his platoon: Lieutenant Shepard cried out, horrified. He could not hear his own shout of despair. The shells had taken his hearing and his men.

In the flaming light and silence he saw men running forward. He saw sheets of mud rise up to splatter the sky. Great contorted branches were blown off the trees. A hundred rifles spat whitely into the gloom.

Rocks and uniforms caught redly on fire. The shadows of men continued to fall. They somersaulted and slithered in the mud. Other shadows rushed unstoppably into the dawn. Their rifles led them on without care. The noise of war was thunderous, but for Lieutenant Shepard the battle had no sound. Time seemed slowed or running backward, or finishing.

The Lieutenant heard chiming: his hearing returned. No-man's-land boiled in unholy chaos. He heard berserk shouting, shrieks of outrage and dismay. He heard the untamed whinnying of terrified warhorses. He heard piteous cries of agony, and artillery shrilling through the air. Mostly he heard the rifles, and the sodden thud of shadows collapsing into the mud.

Then he heard something else: a soft sound, behind him. "Lieutenant. Lieutenant."

He craned to see over his shoulder. Hunched at his feet was a young man. Blood was washing from him, drenching his uniform. The Lieutenant struggled to remember the boy's name, but only his first would come – Ernie. The special thing about Ernie was that he worked in his family's bicycle repair shop. He had told Lieutenant Shepard that, should he ever have a wobbly bicycle, Ernie would fix it without charge.

"Lieutenant. Lieutenant." Ernie was trembling, fluttering his hands. The Lieutenant looked away from him, across the battlefield. The stump of a tree was torn up and tossed into the sky. Daggers of its splintered wood cut the air like circus knives. Clods of earth showered from its tortured roots. In the distance a man was standing, encouraging the soldiers on. His arms spun like loosed windmill blades. Then he fell.

"Lieutenant. Lieutenant."

The Lieutenant glanced impatiently at Ernie. Be quiet! he wanted to say. He wanted to tell the dying boy to

have the decency to die in silence. Couldn't he see that the Lieutenant had other things to think about?

And when he heard these hideous thoughts in his head, the Lieutenant was ashamed. He pictured Ernie's father crouched beside a spinning bicycle wheel. Soon a telegram would arrive at the door of the repair shop, and Ernie's father would always wonder about the last moments of his son's life. The Lieutenant could not let this boy fade into the mud, his final words unheard.

He wriggled around on his belly, keeping his head down. He brought his face close to the boy's. "What is it, Ernie?"

"I'm not hurt." Ernie's voice was hot and dry. His teeth were stained pink. "I'm not hurt."

He mumbled something that was lost beneath the screech of artillery shells. The Lieutenant shielded the boy's face as soil and shrapnel sprayed down. The sky flamed with violent colour. The boy was shivering.

"What is it, Ernie?" the soldier asked again.

The boy drew a rattling breath. "In my pocket."

The soldiers carried keepsakes in the breast pockets of their uniforms, close to their hearts. Lucky charms and photographs, locks of hair and pressed flowers from home. In times of danger they wanted these things near. The Lieutenant moved to unbutton Ernie's pocket. At his touch, the boy yelled. A chorus of woeful cries answered him, echoing across the field. The Lieutenant saw that he'd become smudged with Ernie's blood. Ernie bucked and quivered. "My pocket," he insisted. "My pocket."

The Lieutenant heard a frenzied shout, and bullets rocketed past his ears. He covered his head with his arms desperately – the end had come, as he'd known it would. He mumbled anguished prayers and curses, his eyes filling with tears. He did not want – he'd never wanted – to die.

The next moment, the shelling stopped.

The air seemed to peal with the abrupt quiet. The

Lieutenant looked up cautiously, staring into the mist. He saw shadows shaped like soldiers rising from the ground. The Lieutenant watched them, and his flesh crawled in horror. The shadows rising from the mud were the shape of the enemy.

"Pocket. Pocket."

The shadows rose like towers, tall and straight as titans. They walked across no-man's-land with massive, brazen strides. They walked apart, like crows in a cornfield. They paused beside groaning bundles on the ground. They prodded bundles with their boots. Their bayonets flared in the dawn.

"Pocket."

The Lieutenant saw a titan turn, having heard the voice. His blue and black rifle see-sawed at his side. The Lieutenant clamped a hand on Ernie's mouth, but the giant had heard. He came, out of the greyness, towards the gutter where the soldiers lay.

The Lieutenant kept his hand on Ernie's mouth. The boy struggled without strength. He wanted to say *Look in my pocket, Lieutenant. There's something there I can't live without.*

The Lieutenant heard mud squelch beneath the titan's boots, heard the man's gruff breathing. He was close now, close, close. There was no time left to do anything; nothing, now, could be changed. In the next second, the enemy soldier would loom above the gutter and gaze down on them.

The Lieutenant relaxed into the mud. He let himself sink. He felt his hand, relaxing, slip down Ernie's cheek. He kept his eyes open. He was covered in blood. He prayed that he looked like a lifeless shadow on the ground.

He held his breath. His heart beat lonesomely on.

The giant was there suddenly, on the edge of the gutter.

The Lieutenant's heart paused.

'In my pocket!" said Ernie.

The giant's bayonet flashed down. The Lieutenant did not blink.

He lay motionless for what felt like hours. Even when the titans were gone and the field was soundless, he continued to lie still. He felt the mud creeping up his legs. He felt himself growing cold. Ernie, beside him, was very cold. The Lieutenant's eyes ached, and he shut them. Then opened them again quickly, afraid of the dark.

A longer time passed. The Lieutenant shivered. A gust of rain blew from the sky; later the clouds parted, and the Lieutenant glimpsed mellow blue.

Only when a raven landed nearby did he climb stiffly to his knees.

No-man's-land looked exactly as he'd thought it would. The few trees still standing were ugly as witch's claws. The field was a leafless, lifeless boneyard of mud. Fingers of barbed wire scratched the air. Fat flies bumbled near the ground.

The Lieutenant looked at Ernie. The boy's pocket was securely buttoned. With shaking hands the Lieutenant unfastened it. He envisioned ghosts and souls spilling free. Instead, inside the pocket was a photograph. Some soldiers carried pictures of sweethearts or wives. Some carried photos of faithful dogs. Ernie's photograph showed a tidy shopfront. On the doorstep of the shop stood a man, a woman and two girls. Beside them was propped a bicycle. Above the doorway of the shop were painted the words WHITTAKER'S BICYCLE REPAIRS. Ernie's name was Ernest Whittaker. It was good to remember. The people in the photograph were Ernie's parents and sisters. His younger sister was sucking her thumb. His mother looked bashfully aside. His father was standing proud as a lion. The Lieutenant tucked the photograph in Ernie's hand.

He rose unsteadily to his feet. He stretched and rubbed his chill legs. Then he began to walk home.

He had meant to stop walking when he

reached the allied lines. The Lieutenant believed that, when he found the trenches, he would stop, claim a rifle, be a soldier at war once again. Instead, at the trenches, he realized he had further to walk. He had miles of countryside and sea to cross before he reached home.

Somebody, seeing how pale he looked, handed him a blanket. He should have lain down underneath it and slept, but he didn't. He found his haversack where he'd left it, and slung it over a shoulder. He might yet have stopped, but he didn't – he kept walking. Amid the shooting and shouting and detonating shells, no one noticed he'd gone.

Nor did anyone notice Ernest Whittaker had gone.

When he'd walked several miles and evening had drawn down, the soldier reached in his pocket for his compass. His pocket held the compass, a box of raisins and a letter from his mother, and something else – something that had been forgotten. He fished out the forgotten thing and struck a match to see it. The silver donkey gazed peacefully at him through the soft light of the flame.

And the soldier had sat down and sobbed then, so happy was he to be going home.

THEIR
CAMPAIGN BEGINS

AT breakfast the following morning the children's mother said, "I don't know where all the food is going. I'm sure there was cheese in the cupboard yesterday."

"Maybe we've got mice, Mama!" suggested Marcelle. "They're sneaking into the kitchen while we're asleep, and eating all our food."

"Maybe we should get a cat, Mama?" said Coco, who wanted a pet.

"I think Marcelle is right," replied their mother. "I think we do have mice in the house. Only they're not small and furry, with big ears and long tails. The mice we have in this house are the shape of greedy children!"

Pascal, Marcelle and Coco glanced at one another. They knew they had to be careful, and protect the soldier in the woods. "It was me, Mama," said Pascal. "I ate the cheese. I am always hungry."

"Maybe Pascal's got worms, Mama," proposed Coco maliciously.

"Shut up Thérèse!" said her brother. "You've got worms for a *brain*!"

"At least I don't *look* like a worm! You do!"

"Be quiet, both of you," sighed their mother. "You must be growing, Pascal, if you're hungry all the time. Thank goodness there's only one boy in the house, and not an entire army. We couldn't afford to feed you."

"I'm sorry, Mama. I'll try to stop growing."

"But can we still get a cat?" Coco asked.

The children had dragged their feet that morning, and now they were running late for school. Their mother pushed them out the door and pleaded with them to hurry, fearing Madame Hugo's cold opinion of parents whose children were tardy. Pascal, Marcelle and Coco trotted through the cobbled lanes, their satchels bouncing on their backs. "Monsieur Lieutenant missed breakfast again," said Marcelle regretfully, but they weren't as worried as they might have been, for they knew that their soldier was strong. Nevertheless Pascal seemed deep in thought, and when the lanes brought them to the village and they could see, at a distance, the flint walls and chimney-pots of the school house, he suddenly stopped walking, and his sisters looked at him. "The situation is dire," he announced importantly. "Mama is asking too many questions. Soon she will become suspicious. It's time to put the rescue campaign into operation."

"What rescue campaign?" Marcelle asked. "You haven't told us anything, Pascal."

"Yes, and we found the soldier first!" said Coco.

In truth, Pascal did not need the assistance of his sisters. His brilliant rescue campaign could succeed without their help. But Pascal was a boy who liked things to be fair and square: deep inside, he did not like to be spiteful or mean. He didn't want to break his sisters' hearts by leaving them out of the excitement. He ducked into the shade of the glass-blower's awning, and beckoned them to huddle near. As quickly and quietly as he could, he told Marcelle and Coco the details of his plan. While Coco listened, she chewed her lip; Marcelle nodded seriously. At the end of the explanation Pascal asked, "So, what do you think?"

Coco looked at Marcelle. "I'm not sure," said Marcelle. "I wish we didn't have to tell anyone else about Monsieur Lieutenant."

"But we have to trust somebody." Coco took her sister's hand. "Otherwise, what can we do?"

Marcelle nodded ruefully. Coco was right. Without help, they couldn't do anything. "I think it's a good idea, Pascal," she said.

"So do I!" chirped Coco.

"Well!" said Pascal, puffing his chest. "We should hurry! The Lieutenant can't stay in the woods forever."

"No," said Coco, "he needs to go home! His poor brother John is calling for him."

"We must help him escape before somebody finds him, and sends him back to the war."

Coco clapped her hands to her face at the thought. "Would they, Pascal? Could they?"

"Of course!"

Marcelle said, "Then you're right – we must hurry. We need to rescue the soldier as soon as we can. Run, Pascal – run!"

The three children parted at a gallop. Marcelle and Coco raced to the school house. Madame Hugo frowned as they burst through the door. "You are late!" she thundered. "Where is your brother?"

"At the dairy with Papa," fibbed Coco shamelessly. "There was trouble with a cow."

But Pascal was in fact racing through the village streets, past sturdy brick shopfronts and gaily painted doors, past buckets of geraniums and the rugged old clocktower, and flying down the hundred ageless stone steps that led to the harbour, the fishing boats, and the broad green sea.

LIEUTENANT SHEPARD SEES

THAT evening the soldier heard a familiar whistle, and looked up through the trees. It had been a long and strange day for him. He had kept the silver donkey hidden in his hand. Holding it made him feel protected while he thought back on the war. Having its small weight in his palm made him feel less alone.

Something else had happened: his sight had returned. It was only very slightly restored – he still saw a blotted whiteness everywhere – but within the whiteness he could now see frail silhouettes. He could see the outlines of branches and leaves shifting against the sky. Pascal's whistle was accompanied by four slender, indistinct shapes which walked within the whiteness like angels inside clouds.

The soldier heard rough laughter, and words spoken in a voice he didn't know. "Ah!" said the voice. *"Donc vous n'êtes pas l'invention du garçon!"*

The soldier's heart quickened with anxiety. A stranger in the forest made him feel very nervous. He smiled bravely, however. "Yes, I am real. Pascal did not invent me."

"Bonjour, Lieutenant," said the stranger. "My name is Fabrice. I am proud and honoured to meet you. I am an old friend of Coco, Marcelle and Pascal. They think I can be of assistance to you."

"Monsieur Lieutenant," piped up Coco, "I am here." She did not want him thinking he was alone with somebody he didn't know.

"I am here too," said Pascal quickly.

"And me," said Marcelle. "We're sorry we couldn't come sooner. Papa made us help him wash out the dairy, and Fabrice could not come here until he had finished work. I know you must be hungry. We've brought you some food. It isn't much, I'm afraid. There's olives and two boiled eggs, and a jug of milk from the dairy."

"And I have brought a bottle of beer," added Fabrice. "I thought that, if you were imaginary, I could always drink it myself."

The children sat down around the soldier. Fabrice leaned against a tree. The soldier's eyesight was not repaired enough to see that Fabrice, although a young man, had the weak bent legs of an old man. When he was a boy, Fabrice had contracted polio. The muscles in his legs had been damaged, and wasted away. Walking with the children across the fields and through the forest had left him fatigued, though he would never say so.

Marcelle peeled the eggs and gave them to the soldier. He could not hold the eggs and the silver donkey at the same time. "Coco," he said.

Coco's hand flashed out. The silver donkey jumped onto her palm. It ran around in circles, braying, and kicked its matchstick legs. Coco saw herself shrunk tiny, riding on its back. The tiny girl and the little donkey cantered over the hills, past tawny cows and quacking ducks and Mama, who was astonished, and Papa, who was amazed. Clutching handfuls of tussled coat, Coco let the donkey run far and fast as he could.

Fabrice was saying something. "Pascal has told me your story, Lieutenant Shepard. I know you have walked away from the war. I know you're travelling home to see your brother. I know you need to cross the Channel. I know you cannot see."

The soldier nodded, and did not speak, and took a bite of egg. He did not tell Fabrice that his eyesight was returning. He thought Fabrice would laugh at the

notion that the war had been such a horrifying sight that his eyes had stopped wanting to see, but that the time spent here, in the cool cradle of the forest, was restoring their faith in the beauty of the world. He could tell this to Coco and Marcelle and Pascal, but a grown-up would probably laugh. The soldier knew he had no choice but to trust Fabrice, for he needed an adult's help. But things felt changed and more perilous, now a man stood in the woods.

"We all have our problems," Fabrice was musing. "I have some of my own. My legs are wobbly as a puppet's. I scrub barnacles off fishing boats while my friends become heroes in the war. I cannot even ask my *amoureuse* to marry me, because I can't afford a wedding ring. It's not right – is it? – to ask a girl to marry a man who can't give her a wedding ring. I dream, at night, of a wedding ring that would make an empress jealous. I see the diamonds and the engraving, I see it glittering in the sun. I wake up determined

to sell everything I own, in order to buy my sweetheart this ring. But the only thing I own is my motorcycle, and that I cannot sell. I need it; it is my livelihood. The motorcycle is what I have instead of useful legs."

The soldier had finished both eggs by the time Fabrice concluded his speech. He thought that having wobbly legs and no wedding ring were small worries compared with being blind and marooned in a forest. He thought that scrubbing barnacles off boats sounded quite an agreeable way to pass the days – better than sloshing about in trenches and scraping mud off boots. But he had been brought up to be polite, and to respect the feelings of others. "Yes," he said, "we each have our problems."

Pascal, meanwhile, was bored. He thought barnacles and wedding rings exceptionally tedious things. He'd been idly picking twigs and leaves from the soldier's grubby blanket. Now he said, "Lieutenant, tell us about the war. What is it like? Exciting, I bet."

Coco and the silver donkey stopped galloping and

looked back the way they'd come, over miles of rustling forest and sunny, shining hills. The soldier's blue eyes were resting on her. She smiled and waved at him.

Marcelle said, "You don't have to tell us anything, if remembering makes you sad."

But the soldier said, "If Pascal wants badly to hear a story about the war, I know the story I will tell."

Pascal grinned, and made himself more comfortable on the ground. Marcelle stretched out beside him, her chin in her hands. Fabrice pulled the cap from the bottle of beer and passed the bottle to the soldier. Coco twitched the silver donkey's mane and charged off towards the hills.

THE THIRD TALE

THE boy was born in a seaside town. His family wasn't rich, but they were happy. The boy spent his days roaming the streets and countryside with his friends. At the docks there were giant, fabulous creatures of steel; beyond the town were dark mines from which the sounds of the underworld clanked and boomed. Mostly there was the beach, where crabs could be caught and castles built and where, in the high season, cheerful holiday-makers flocked to bathe their pale bodies in the sun. The holiday-makers' children clamoured for rides on the donkeys which walked up and down the sand. The donkeys wore coloured saddles and straw hats trimmed with ribbon; a ride cost tuppence. To earn some pocket money, the boy asked the donkey-keeper for a job tending the donkeys. Until now, he'd never given much thought to donkeys. He found that he liked the quiet, docile beasts. He liked the wheaten smell of them and their deep, considering eyes. He liked the way their ears turned like quick, limber canoes. In library books he discovered that donkeys came in different colours and breeds. The breeds had fancy names like Poitou, Anatolian, and Grey Provençal. The boy's name was simply Jack. When the high season was over, he was sorry to see the donkeys taken away to a sunnier beach elsewhere.

As time passed and Jack grew older, donkeys left his mind. Instead he farewelled his family and caught a boat across the ocean. He travelled in search of

adventure. He found himself in a hot country on the other side of the world. For a time, he was happy. He became rugged and brown. He was a larrikin, a joker, and everyone liked him. After a few years, however, Jack grew homesick. He wanted to see his old mum again. But he had no money, and it was too far to swim. He began to think he might never see his mother and father, his sisters and brothers, his childhood home again.

Then something happened: war was declared. Jack was delighted, and immediately joined up. The war was being fought on the other side of the world – exactly where Jack wanted to go. The soldiers would be given a free boat ride there. Jack's problem was solved. Soon he'd be drinking tea with his mum.

He was given a uniform and put on a ship. The ship crossed the ocean in the direction of Jack's home – but as they came closer, the ship changed course, chugging along the beams of sunlight that reflected off the sea. When the captain shut the engines and announced that they'd arrived, Jack looked over the ship's railing and saw steep grey cliffs rising like a fortress from the waves. The cliffs were matted with thorny scrub, and scarred with ridges and gullies. At their base was a line of white sand; above them spread a blue sky. The soldiers were told they must climb these cliffs, which were the only route to the foreign fields beyond. But at the peak of the cliffs were camped the enemy. From their vantage point they would have a perfect view of anyone scrambling up the heights. Accordingly, the enemy had trained their guns to overlook the water and the cliffs.

Jack had been made a stretcher-bearer, because he was fast and strong. When he looked at the cliffs and the enemy camps at their peak, he knew the stretcher-bearers were going to be busy. Many soldiers would fall in the struggle to scale the cliffs. Many soldiers would not even reach the beach alive.

But some did manage to swarm part-way up the cliffs. The enemy fired on them relentlessly. The

injured stumbled and slid on the rocks. Machine-guns peppered bullets through the air. Men screamed with anger and fear. The noise was tremendous and deafening. Soldiers tumbled down the cliffs like stones.

The army commanders saw that it was impossible to reach the peak. They ordered the soldiers to dig in while they thought up a better plan. The men dug trenches as fast as lightning. Compared to stumbling around on the cliffs, the trenches were safe as houses. The men clustered together, praying the commanders would rescue them from the dreadful trap they were in.

But the commanders did nothing of the sort. They worried that, should they abandon the cliffs, the enemy would think they were running away. So the soldiers stayed in the trenches, and the enemy sat at the clifftops and rained bullets down on them.

Within the first handful of days, two thousand men fell.

Jack, a stretcher-bearer, spent the time running up and down the cliffs. The stretcher-bearers' task was to

transport injured soldiers to the beach, from where they would be ferried out to waiting hospital boats. The stretcher-bearers would deliver a patient, then climb the cliffs again. As they climbed, they ducked bullets and flying shrapnel. At the line of fighting there were always many men lying hurt. The stretcher-bearers couldn't transport all the injured at once, and sometimes they had no choice but to leave the wounded waiting and waiting for help. The stretcher-bearers soon realized that the unwieldy stretchers were slowing them down. They tossed the stretchers aside and began carrying the injured to the beach. A strong young man like Jack could sling a soldier over his shoulder and sprint down the cliffs like a gazelle. He could lay the soldier on the beach and be back at the trenches in minutes.

Rescuing the wounded became Jack's reason for

being on the cliffs, his reason for staying alive. Over and around the rocks he ran like a hare. He carried soldiers on his shoulders all day and into the night. Sometimes he stumbled, and his wounded passenger cried out. Sometimes he felt his strength waning for lack of water and good food. He worried about becoming too weak to save the men who needed saving.

Then one day, when Jack was hastening along a path that snaked secretly up the cliff, his eye was caught by a small grey shadow beside a patch of scrub. A donkey was standing there, nibbling the leaves. Donkeys had travelled on the same ships as the soldiers: they were used to haul supplies. Usually they were tethered, but this one had escaped. Jack gazed at the donkey, watching it placidly eat. It was entirely untroubled by the danger and the noise. Jack remembered how, as a boy, he'd led donkeys on the beach. How good and sweet-natured those animals had been! How stoic and enduring! The noble donkey family-tree came rushing back to his mind. The brown

Cotentin, with its snowy nose, and the long-haired Poitou, which was scruffy and wild. The Anatolian's coat was the colour of stones; the Grey Provençal bore a remembrance cross. Donkeys, Jack knew, were trustworthy, sure-footed, and willing to please. A donkey could bear wounded soldiers down precarious cliffs and it would rarely stumble and hardly tire. With a donkey at his side, Jack could rescue many more men than he was rescuing on his own. He grabbed the rope hanging from the donkey's halter and brought the animal to the nearest hurt soldier. He helped the man onto the donkey's back, and put an arm around his shoulders. Then the three of them – Jack, his patient, and the donkey – made their way down to the beach. They dodged bullets and shrapnel and holes in the ground. Soldiers, seeing them, stared in surprise. Jack, smelling the donkey's rustic scent, remembered the town where he was born, the sunshine, sand and sea.

From that day on there was always a donkey at Jack's side. The man and the animal worked together as a team. They scoured the scrubby cliffs for men in need of aid. The donkey would carry the patient while Jack navigated a safe path through the battle. As soon as they laid the man on the beach they'd be back among the rubble, running to the next needy soul. They learned every dip and dent of the land. Though bullets and shrapnel and snipers were everywhere, Jack and his donkey weren't touched. Jack never seemed afraid. He never hesitated. He was as calm and resilient as the animal beside him.

Jack took excellent care of the donkey. Each day he scrounged fresh fodder for it. He rested only when he thought the donkey might be weary. While he rested, he fretted about the injured soldiers who needed him. He knew that they were scanning the cliffs for sight of the man and the donkey.

A wounded soldier on the donkey's back would sometimes find strength to ask, "What's your donkey called, Jack?"

Jack would smile and answer, "Well, you know, I'm

too busy to think up a name – perhaps you've got an idea?"

And while Jack, the donkey and the patient picked their way down the cliff, the soldier would try out various names that might suit a little donkey. The soldiers often chose names that reminded them of fine times before the war. "Flashfire," one might say, "was the name of a racehorse that no other horse could beat. I once won three quid on him! You should call your donkey Flashfire, Jack."

"All right," Jack would agree. "Flashfire it is."

Another soldier might say, "Call this donkey Nipper, Jack. I've got a dog at home called Nipper."

Jack would mull on it and eventually say, "Yes, Nipper is the best name."

Another soldier suggested, "Buttons. When I was a boy on the farm, we had a donkey named Buttons. Buttons is the proper name for a donkey."

"I like that name, Buttons," Jack would say. "Tell me about your farm."

The donkey reminded everyone of good things and better times. "Call him Billy, after my brother, who had the biggest ears. How we used to tease the poor bugger, Jack." "Call your donkey Greystoke, Jack. That's the name of my grandmammy's house. The pies she used to bake, Jack! The glorious smell of them!" Soon the donkey had earned itself a hundred different names. Even Jack was christened with an extra one. The soldiers began to call him "the bravest of the brave'. And, because the donkey reminded them of better times, the soldiers began to feel optimistic, exactly as they'd felt in those better times. When they saw Jack and his donkey, the soldiers remembered they weren't alone. They trusted that Jack would save them if they were injured and fell. They knew that he would pick them up, bandage them up, and carry them off to safety.

Being near the donkey made Jack feel better too. The downy grey fur reminded him of summer on the slate roofs of his town. The trim black hooves reminded him of the square cobbles in the street. The warm scent of the donkey reminded Jack of his mother's kitchen. In his mind's eye he saw her standing on the front step, calling him in for tea.

For twenty-four days and nights Jack and his donkey trod the cliffside. The donkey stood steady while Jack tended an injured man. It carried each patient carefully, never stumbling or shying. Bullets flew around Jack and his donkey, but never touched them. The soldiers began to wonder whether the enemy, perched where they could see everything, had also seen the donkey, and had remembered better times. Maybe the enemy were cautious when the donkey was near, because they didn't want to hurt it – they wanted to keep remembering.

But war is war, and sometimes soldiers forget that there are good things, things worth keeping, in the world.

One morning Jack and the donkey climbed a ridge to reach a man who was crying out for help. Jack was

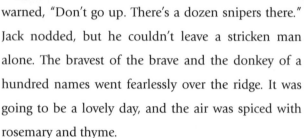

warned, "Don't go up. There's a dozen snipers there." Jack nodded, but he couldn't leave a stricken man alone. The bravest of the brave and the donkey of a hundred names went fearlessly over the ridge. It was going to be a lovely day, and the air was spiced with rosemary and thyme.

The wounded man was lying in a patch of open ground. Jack remembered the warning about snipers being nearby. The open ground looked like a dangerous place to be. "Stay here," he told the donkey, and pushed it back amidst the scrub. He liked to keep the donkey as safe as it could be. Then he dashed out across the open land, running fast as the wind.

But a bullet struck him anyway, and he tumbled to the ground. The breeze whipped up a gritty whirligig that blew across his face.

Jack knew that he was badly injured, and that he wouldn't live. He closed his eyes against the garish

blueness of the sky. He heard distant gunfire, and the whistling of bullets. He heard soldiers shouting that the bravest of the brave had fallen.

Then he felt something touch his face. Jack hadn't the strength to open his eyes. But he knew that the donkey had left the bushes and come to him, and had lowered its grey face to his own. Its soft muzzle had brushed his cheek as delicately as velvet. He smelt its rustic, dusty scent. The smell made Jack think of home.

His mother was calling him in for supper, and Jack, dying, ran to her.

HEROES

THE soldier's audience was quiet at the end of this story. Each was thinking about Jack and the war. Coco looked at the silver donkey and imagined it carrying wounded soldiers to the beach. She had always thought of war as a strange shaded place where men argued crossly and frequently played cards. She could not imagine hot scrubby cliffs which soldiers tumbled down like stones.

Pascal, though, was roaming the rocky battlefield in

his mind. His eyes had widened with every mention of bullets and shrapnel and peril. He could hardly imagine anything more exciting. He pretended he hadn't heard the end of the story – when Jack had died.

Fabrice had heard it, though. He admired Jack's bravery, and envied him for having had the chance to prove it. Fabrice wanted desperately to do something courageous in his life. He did not want to limp behind everyone else forever.

Marcelle stayed thoughtful for the longest time. Her eyes had tears in them. Jack's story had filled her with love and pity for all things. She swore that she would devote herself to doing what was good. She would try to help the suffering. She would try to turn wrong into right.

"Are you still there?" asked the soldier, though he could see their blurry shapes.

"We're here," Pascal assured him. "We were just thinking."

"Yesterday you thought you knew a way for me to

get home," said the soldier. "Will you tell me what it is, Pascal?"

"It is a fine plan," said Fabrice. "I think it will work."

The soldier struggled to see the boy through the lingering fog in his eyes. Evening was creeping through the woods like a cat, and for the first time in many days the soldier could see a hint of night's black flank. His eyesight was returning – but slowly, slowly, as if hardly wanting to be there. He said, "Tell me the plan, Pascal."

Pascal sat up importantly, and explained his idea. The soldier listened carefully. He interrupted now and then, and asked several questions. Sometimes Fabrice broke in to tell the soldier this and that. Marcelle listened closely, and marvelled that an ordinary girl such as she could be responsible for starting an entire adventure.

Coco also listened, although she didn't want to. She wanted the soldier to be happy and she was concerned about poor sick John, but nevertheless she did not want the soldier to go home. She knew that, once the soldier was gone, the forest would seem empty and sad.

Pascal and Fabrice reached the end of their explanation. The soldier said nothing, thinking about the plan. He knew he could invent no better scheme himself. "When would we do this?" he asked.

"Tomorrow night," said Fabrice. "Friday is always the quietest night in the village."

"Tomorrow!" Coco objected, and everyone looked at her. "Tomorrow is too soon!"

Marcelle said gently, "Remember, Coco, that Monsieur is not safe here. He needs to get away. And his brother John is watching, waiting for him to come home."

Coco nodded reluctantly, clutching the silver donkey. When she thought about the empty forest, her eyelids fluttered and her chin wiggled and she wanted to howl.

"Tomorrow night then," said the soldier. "Very well. I shall be ready."

Fabrice's legs were aching. They ached when he stood a long time. He wanted to sit down but he worried that, if he did, he might not look valiant. He wanted the children to think of him as dauntless and in command. Fabrice couldn't imagine captains and generals sitting on a damp forest floor. He looked into the sky and said, "Night's coming, children – time for you to go home. Hurry, before your papa comes searching. I'll stay here a minute, to speak with the Lieutenant."

Marcelle, Pascal and Coco climbed ponderously to their feet. "Good night, Monsieur," said Coco, slipping the silver donkey into the soldier's hand. The three of them walked away slowly, casting resentful glances back at Fabrice. In the children's opinion, Lieutenant Shepard belonged to them – after all, they had found him. They had been nice enough to tell Fabrice about him. Now Fabrice was stealing the soldier because they were just children, and inconsequential, and there was nothing they could do to stop him. It made them sulky and peevish. As well-brought-up children, however, they could not scold Fabrice; instead they scolded each other all the way down the hill.

Fabrice, meanwhile, was sitting down, and sighing in blessed relief. He was thankful that the soldier was blind and couldn't see him looking ungallant. "May I ask you some questions, Lieutenant?" he said.

"Of course," answered the soldier.

"Pascal has told me about your ill brother – John," Fabrice began. "Do you really have a brother, Lieutenant? Is he really ill? Or is he a ghost made of wishes and fear, someone you invented to disguise your shame in fleeing a war which other men, braver men, have stayed behind to fight?"

The soldier grimly smiled. "What difference does it make," he asked, "if my brother is real or not? I have still run away from the war. I have still done a shameful, cowardly thing."

"If the army catches you, they will shoot you for desertion."

The soldier knew this, and said nothing.

Fabrice added, "Perhaps they also shoot those who help soldiers to desert."

The soldier thought this could be true. He said, "I don't want to put you in danger, Fabrice. I would understand if you decided the risk was too great."

Fabrice looked down at his crooked legs. "Life demands we take risks sometimes," he replied. "I wanted to be a soldier but the army would not take me, because of my legs. A man doesn't need legs to fire a gun; battles are won with brains, not legs. But the army turned me away, and since then I have felt worthless. No one, I thought, needs me, no one will ever want my help. Then Pascal told me about you. You need help, Lieutenant, and I want to help you. Better than that, I can help you. I don't care if it's dangerous. You are blind, you are tired, you have done your best – now you long to go home. You deserve to go home. I will help you get there, and then I'll know that I, too, can do something worthwhile."

The soldier was silent. His head was bowed. "I am grateful to you."

"Don't be," Fabrice answered. "I do this for me, as much as for you."

"The boat, the fuel – these things will cost money. Yet you cannot afford a wedding ring for your sweetheart…"

Fabrice shook his head. "Don't say this, Lieutenant!"

"My pockets are empty," the soldier continued, holding the silver donkey in his hand. The donkey was crafted from the finest metal. It was silver to its core. The soldier supposed it was worth some money. He said, "If you will let me, I will give –"

Fabrice interrupted loudly, "Lieutenant! It's not often in life that a man gets the chance to do something heroic. Don't spoil it for me by talking about something as uncouth as money!"

The soldier smiled bleakly. "Very well." He gazed, unseeing, at the donkey. "Tomorrow night, then," he sighed. "I will be here, waiting."

"Good. The boat will be ready." Fabrice got to his feet. "I will pack a basket and bring my violin. With music and food and a flagon of wine, our voyage will be a pleasant one! Good night, my friend, sleep well."

The soldier listened as the young man hobbled away. He thought back on all that he'd been told. He believed he could trust Fabrice. It was the rescue plan which bothered him. The situation was dangerous and complicated: yet the plan was utterly simple. Beneath the soldier's enthusiasm for the plan lay a deep dread that it would not work – that, somehow, its very simplicity would make it fail. He hoped and prayed he was wrong: hoping and praying was all he could do.

He leaned back against his tree and drew the blanket around him. He sensed that the evening had grown dark now. A breeze was brushing through the branches leisurely. Woodpigeons were shaking daylight from their feathers and tucking their heads beneath their wings. At night, the forest was tranquil. The trees whispered mellowly to each other. Some creatures dozed; others walked softly about. Diamonds of water gathered on the newly unfolded spring leaves. At night, the forest was wildness at rest. The soldier was glad to be going home, but he would never forget the forest.

THE LAST AFTERNOON

THE children could scarcely concentrate in school the next day. Pascal burned in anticipation of the evening's escapade. Marcelle thought about it too, worrying that something would go wrong. Coco thought wistfully of many things: of the war, and the empty forest. She did not hear Madame Hugo ask, "What is the name of England's Prime Minister?" She gazed out the window with a heavy heart.

When Madame Hugo rang the bell at the end of the day, Pascal raced away to the docks. He wanted to find Fabrice and check that everything was going to plan. Marcelle and Coco walked slowly home. "I wish we had money to buy the soldier a pastry," said Marcelle. "We can pick some flowers for him instead."

Coco turned her face up to her sister. "Marcie," she murmured, "why is Papa not fighting the war, like that man Jack was, and Monsieur Lieutenant?"

"Well, because somebody must stay behind to milk the cows."

Coco dawdled, considering this. She said, "I would be frightened if Papa was fighting the war."

"Me too," said Marcelle.

At home, the shelves of the pantry looked bare. The sisters found a corner of bread and a small pot of honey. "Maybe he'll be too happy to be hungry," said Marcelle.

They walked hand-in-hand along the lane, then climbed the emerald-green hills. As they climbed, they picked the wildflowers which bloomed amid the grass.

Soon they had bright handfuls of violets and anemone. The sun shone warmly down as they walked. Insects flew buzzing from the grass.

As they went into the woods Coco asked, "Shall we use Pascal's whistle?"

Marcelle tried the whistle. She made a noise like a hen. "The whistle is stupid," she said curtly. "We'll just call out to him, like we always did."

The soldier heard them coming before he saw them. During the day, his eyesight had cleared more than he'd dared hope it would. He could see shadowy images of the trees. He could see their lean branches and their leaves riding the breeze. His vision was weak and fuzzy, as if he saw things from under water, but he saw colours, he saw sky, he thought that, when he'd crossed the Channel, he'd be able to see the road that would lead to his home. When he heard footsteps in the forest, the soldier looked up and saw two girls wearing blue chequered dresses. In their arms they carried flowers that smelled of the sun and the hills.

"It's us, Monsieur," said the taller child. "Marcelle and Coco."

"I can almost see you," said the soldier.

The sisters paused, feeling shy. "Can you see my hair that looks like a poodle's?" asked Coco.

"I can," said the soldier. "Except I think it's prettier than a poodle's could ever be."

Coco giggled. Marcelle rolled her eyes. She said, "We brought some bread and honey for you. There was nothing else."

"Bread and honey sounds delicious," said the soldier. "I don't know what would have happened if you hadn't found me, Marcelle. You have saved my life."

Marcelle blushed and smiled, and both girls felt happy. They sat down close to their soldier. Marcelle drizzled honey over the bread. Coco showed the soldier the flowers they'd brought. The soldier searched his pocket for the silver donkey, and handed it to Coco without waiting to be asked.

Marcelle watched the soldier eat the bread hungrily.

She said, "You must be pleased to be going home tonight."

The soldier nodded. "I *am* pleased. But I will also miss the forest."

Marcelle looked around at the gracious elms and spreading beech. "Aren't there forests where you come from, Lieutenant?"

The soldier smiled. "Yes, there are. But at home I live in a house. At home, I don't live in the woods. They would think I was mad if I did."

"People would tease you, if you lived in the woods. They'd call you names."

"Monsieur Squirrel!" said Coco.

"Monsieur Badger!" laughed Marcelle.

"Yes, that would happen." The soldier was solemn. "But I have liked living here, in this forest."

"You could stay, if you wanted," said Coco.

Marcelle ignored her. She understood that the soldier couldn't stay. She asked, "What's the first thing you'll do when you get home, Monsieur?"

The soldier had been thinking about this, and he knew what to say. "Have a bath," he answered. "Soap my hair into a big white ball. Trim my toes and brush my teeth. Dry myself with a powdered towel. Then get dressed in my pyjamas and my dressing-gown."

"But what about your brother John? Won't you go to see him? Will you tell him that you've come home now, so he can stop crying at night?"

"Of course I will," said the soldier. "When I'm clean and tidy I'll go to his room. I'll bring a tray of biscuits and two mugs of cocoa. I'll sit on his bed and talk to him about the war. I'll tell him about you and Pascal and Fabrice, about being here in the forest. He'll want to hear everything that's happened to the silver donkey."

"Everything that's happened to my silver donkey?" Coco's eyes went round.

"It was John who found the silver donkey." The soldier looked at her. "It was John who gave the silver donkey to me. So he'll want to know where it went and what it saw and all the things that happened."

"How did John find the donkey?" asked Marcelle.

"I'll tell you," said the soldier. "There's time for one last story."

Marcelle sat cross-legged with her chin in her hands. Coco sat fervidly squeezing the silver donkey. Its pointy ears and matchstick legs bit into her palm. She listened to the story, and she thought about the sick boy on the distant side of the Channel. She imagined the soldier telling the boy about the donkey's adventures. She saw the boy riding the silver donkey on a sunny, sandy beach. The boy and the donkey would gallop away, leaving her, Coco, forlorn.

THE FOURTH TALE

"**MY** brother was a good-fortune child," the soldier began. "For many years my family was just my mother, my father, my sister Catherine, and me, and everyone was happy like that. Then John was born, and we wondered how we could have thought there was enough to life without him.

"John was a beautiful child: snowy-haired and green-eyed, very quiet around the house. When he was a baby, he never cried – he never seemed to think there was anything worth crying about. The world was a marvellous place to him – he loved everybody and everything. And everyone adored him in return, for he was irresistible. Robins did not fly away when he approached them on the lawn. Old ladies with the worst tempers turned sweet as cream-cake when he was near. Fearsome hounds played like pups with him. Shopkeepers snuck him treats. There was something magical about John, and this magic extended everywhere. He could mend small broken things that had been judged unfixable. He could plant a temperamental flower and it would thrive like a weed. You might lose a key and search the house for it: John would find it in a moment. He never spilled things or ruined them, never wanted something he couldn't have. You might think that having a perfect brother would be ghastly for Catherine and me; yet it wasn't. We were proud of him. We were proud, too, of ourselves – that out of all the families in the world John should choose to be part of ours. We felt as if a falling star had landed in our house, as if a spectacular rainbow shared our home and our lives.

"But rainbows fade, and mighty stars burn out. The things that are most worth keeping are the things we must always farewell.

"When John was ten years old, he began to trip over his feet. This was odd – he was usually as graceful as a swan. He would return from his rambles panting for air. He took to sleeping in the afternoon – he who had always hated to waste a minute of the day. His appetite for all things faded; he began to grow thin.

"Mother called for the doctor, who examined John thoroughly. 'It's his heart,' the gentleman announced. 'There's nothing we can do.'

"John's heart was failing him: he'd used up all its strength in ten short years. The doctor said John must stay in bed, but John rebelled. The moment he could, he escaped outside. He was angry, and very afraid. He ran to each of his favourite trees, begging for a scrap of

their everlastingness. He ran to the pond and knelt at its edge, pleading for a drop of water's timelessness. He ran to the stables, where his many pets were kept. He did not know what to ask of the animals. In blind fury and dismay he stumbled across the pastures. He was weeping, stamping his feet, shaking his fists at the sky. He loved the world too much: he could not bear to leave it.

"Distraught, he finally sank to the ground. Hardly knowing what he did, he began to dig. In his confused and fearful mind was the notion that, if he could only dig deep enough, he might dig to a place where the hearts of boys never wore out. He would dig and dig and maybe he would manage to dig his way out of his fate.

"The earth was soft. John gouged it with his hands.

Dirt packed under his fingernails and plastered his clothes. He dug until soil was scattered everywhere. Then the effort of digging took its toll. His bones felt jellied; he struggled to breathe. He did not know it, but his lips were blue. He leaned over the hole he'd made, gasping for air. The hole that had exhausted him was shallow, scarcely deep enough to trip a lamb – scarcely there at all. He had not succeeded – he would never succeed – in escaping destiny. John knew that, even if he dug to China, he couldn't make his heart well.

"Tears of defeat dropped down his cheeks and splashed into the hole. One after another they fell plipping into the dirt. Soon they made a puddle; then they washed aside the soil. Suddenly, through his weeping, John glimpsed something shining in the depths of the hole. Curious, he reached in, and drew out an earth-caked, tear-smudged donkey made of silver.

"He wiped the dirt from the donkey, and stared. He wiped his eyes and stared more. What was a silver donkey doing buried in a pasture? Who had put it there? How long had it lain buried, waiting to be found?

"John knew a lot about animals. Gazing at the silver treasure, he thought about donkeys – the facts he'd read, the stories he'd heard, the things he'd learned from watching creatures of all kinds. He put the donkey in his pocket and walked back towards the house. His poor heart was pounding, he needed to rest. But before he reached the house, John took a detour. He returned to the stables where he kept his pets. He had a tortoise and a kestrel and a witty, fleet fox-cub. He had a family of fieldmice and an owl missing a wing. He had a mad-minded weasel who was caged where the fieldmice couldn't see. John petted each of these, and gave them something to eat. Then he sat in the straw and watched them, contemplating many things.

"He had begged the great trees for longevity. He'd pleaded with the water not to let him die. But John hadn't known what to ask of his beloved animals.

Now he did know: he said, 'Let me be more like you, animals. Let me accept that night always follows day. Let me live each of the days as best I can, and sleep in peace at night.'

"The weasel, the mice, the tortoise, the fox, the owl and the kestrel: all of these looked serenely at John. And John felt his fearful heart grow calm.

"At home he polished the silver donkey, and stood it on his bedside table. From then on, he grew a little weaker each day. Soon he couldn't walk across the fields. Soon he lacked the energy to climb a flight of stairs. A wheelchair was bought for him, so he wouldn't lose the pleasure of being out in the fresh air. His bed and toys were moved to a sunny room downstairs. There, he was close to the busy heart of the house. The silver donkey was propped on the sill of the new bedroom. The dawn glinted off its shining flanks. In winter, when snow fell, the flakes made white reflections on the donkey's glimmering hide. John celebrated his birthday. He wheezed like an old man, and hadn't the strength to blow out the eleven candles on his cake."

The soldier paused. He looked at Marcelle and Coco. "By then," he said, "the war had begun. I signed up to become a soldier. My parents and sister were upset. They knew that many soldiers wouldn't come home from the war. They worried that I'd be wounded, or captured by the enemy. They worried I'd be lost in a strange land, among strangers, far away from home."

Marcelle cried, "You're not among strangers! Coco and I are your friends!"

The soldier smiled. "Yes," he said. "John will be glad. When I'd listened to Mother's and Father's and my sister's concerns, I went to John's bedroom. It was a cold day, I remember, but John's room was very snug. A fire was lit in the fireplace. John lay under colourful quilts. He was thin and so pale. He looked up from a book. 'John,' I said, 'I've enlisted. I'm going to fight in the war.'

"John thought on this. Then he smiled. 'If I were older,' he said, 'I could come with you. Then you wouldn't have to go alone – you would have a friend.'

"'While I'm away, I'll think of you,' I promised him.

"We talked more, and eventually it was time for me to go. I kissed his forehead and said, 'You and I will meet again.'

"'Wait,' said John. 'Take the silver donkey with you. It can be your good-luck charm.'

"'But the silver donkey is yours!' I protested.

"'Now it will be yours,'" he replied. "'Every time you see it, you'll remember to do your best.'"

The soldier went quiet, crumpling leaves in his hands. He said, "At first I didn't understand what John meant – I didn't see how a silver donkey would remind me to do my best. Now, though, I think I understand. I believe I know what John meant."

The girls looked intently at the silver donkey. They did not see it as a lifeless object, but as something living and warm. They thought back on the tales that the soldier had told. They remembered Hazel, the gentle Bethlehem donkey, who used the last of her strength helping those who needed her. They remembered the donkey who stood on the mountain and accepted suffering so that others would not know pain. They remembered the donkey with a hundred names, the sturdy friend of Jack, who proved that the most humble being can have the most courageous heart. They gazed at the soldier, who said, "I fear that John will be sorry he gave the silver donkey to me. The silver donkey belongs to the trustworthy and the brave."

Coco said, "But you are those things, Monsieur Lieutenant! You are trustworthy and brave!"

The soldier said nothing. He looked up through the trees. A misty moon was glowing in the early-evening sky. Jays were quarrelling sharply over places to roost for the night. "It's getting late." He spoke hushly. "By this time tomorrow, I'll be home."

"We will miss you," said Marcelle.

"And I will miss you. I will always think of you. I'll think of you growing older and taller. What will you do, when you've grown up? What do you want to become?"

"I am going to be a nurse," said Marcelle. "I want to do something that's good."

The soldier said, "A nurse is an excellent thing to be. You'll make a wonderful nurse, Marcelle."

"I want to be an explorer!" said Coco grandly. "I will travel all over and discover all sorts of things!"

The soldier said, "I'm certain you will do that, Coco. The world is waiting for you."

The sisters and the soldier smiled at one another. "Go home and try to rest," the soldier told them. "There's a long night ahead of us."

The little girls stood obediently, leaves dropping from their laps. If everything went according to plan they would see their soldier one last time, so they did not say goodbye.

AWAY

WHEN it was dark and past
dinnertime and the
village had closed itself up for the night, Fabrice
started his motorcycle and cruised noisily through the
streets. He took the cobbled lane that led past the
house where Pascal, Marcelle and Coco lived. The children had been straining their ears all evening for the
growl of the motorcycle. When she heard it, Coco's
heart beat hard. She felt both thrilled and dismayed.

They had agreed that Pascal would do the talking. "Papa!" he said. "Fabrice told me there's tiddlers swimming under the pier. Can I go down to the harbour and catch some? They make good bait."

"I don't see why you shouldn't," said their father. He was reading a book.

Marcelle said, "If Pascal's allowed to go to the pier, I'm allowed to go too!"

"And me!" chimed in Coco. "I want to go!"

Pascal objected, "You two never stop talking! You'll scare away the fish!"

"Papa! Tell Pascal we can go!"

Their father clamped his hands to his ears. "Pascal, take your sisters to the harbour! It's the only way I'll get any peace."

"None of you are going anywhere." The children's mother did not look up from her darning. "It's nearly bedtime, and cold outside. The fish will be there in the morning."

The children swapped horrified glances. "No!"

Pascal squawked. "They won't be, Mama! You know nothing about fishing! Tiddlers only come to the surface in moonlight. If I don't catch them now, I never will! Anyway, it's too early to go to bed, and we don't have school in the morning."

"When I was a boy," said their father, "we always had lessons on Saturday morning."

"Oh!" Coco gasped. "How horrible! Why don't *we* have lessons on Saturday, Papa?"

"That's a good question, Coco," said Papa. "There are many chores to be done these days, and not enough grown-ups to do them. Madame Hugo cancelled Saturday lessons because she knows that children don't like school, but they love doing chores!"

Coco gurgled with laughter. "You're so funny, Papa."

"Mama," said Pascal, "if we promise to wake up early and do our chores without even one word of complaint, if we *swear on our lives* to do as we're told – then may we go to the harbour?"

"With not one word of complaint!" marvelled Papa. "How I have longed for that day!"

"We swear, Mama! We swear!"

"Promising to do as they're told!" said their father, and clasped his hands over his heart.

The children's mother sighed. It was four against one. "All right," she said, "you may go. But you will have to wear your coats."

"Yes, Mama, we will!"

The children pulled on their coats quickly, before Mama could change her mind; they took the fishing net from its hook and scampered out the door.

Meanwhile Fabrice was riding his motorcycle through the hills behind town. The moon was a half-circle and cast pale luminance on tree trunks and stones. The road soon petered out, vanishing amid brambles and weeds. Fabrice stopped the motorcycle and turned off its buzzing engine. Without the yellow beam of the headlight, the world became suddenly pitch-dark. Speedily Fabrice lit a lamp, and looked around. He knew where he was and he wasn't afraid, but the countryside seemed very different in the glow of the lamp and the moon. The trees rustled spookily; hidden creatures made strange sounds. The witchy whisper of the leaves sent chills down Fabrice's spine. He turned the flame up a little, and limped resolutely on.

The soldier heard him coming. His hearing was keen as an owl's. His vision, though, was still too weak to see through the blackness of night. Into the whispering dark he called, "Fabrice?"

"*C'est moi*," answered Fabrice.

The lamplight explored the clearing where the soldier sat waiting. The trees seemed to lean forward into the light. They seemed to murmur to one another the news of a stranger in their midst. Fabrice did not like it. "Are you ready?" he asked the soldier.

"I am."

The soldier stood. His hands moved uncertainly in the darkness. Fabrice took his arm. "Do you have everything, Lieutenant?"

"Yes," the soldier answered, "I do."

The lame man and the sightless man helped each other down the hill. They travelled slowly, shambling through the dark. The soldier heard the voice of the trees grow distant as woodland gave way to field. Without trees to fragment it, the breeze blew cool and strong. A thread of prickly briar snagged the soldier's trouser hem. Soon he felt pebbles rumbling underneath his boots. Finally the two men reached the road. "Here," said Fabrice. "My motorcycle."

Fabrice helped the soldier fold into the sidecar. The soldier had never ridden in such a thing before. When Fabrice started the motorcycle, the whine and drone of the engine made the soldier wince. It seemed a long time since he'd heard such a loud noise. Loud noise reminded him of the war.

The motorcycle coasted through the hills. They took the narrow low road which weaved past silent farmland. The soldier wore his blanket draped on his head, in the style that old ladies wore hoods. If a farmer searching for lost sheep happened to see them glide by, he'd mistake the soldier for Fabrice's grand'mère.

Nonetheless the soldier kept his head down. He didn't see the hamlets and farmsteads that they passed. He didn't see the blooming groves of apple trees. He didn't see the teetering, weathered picket fences, nor the lanky stands of perfumed pine trees. He didn't see the rocky ruins of the abbey or the scattered remains of the ancient, granite château. He didn't see the river where willows and waterlilies grew, nor the stone bridge which arched prettily across the river's slim

width. Had he seen these beautiful things, he'd scarcely have believed that a terrible war was being fought not far down the road.

The children, in the meantime, were walking through the village. The curving streets were lit by tall wrought-iron lamps. The lamps threw wan beams onto lime-washed walls. The iron handle of a red door creaked with old age. The shingles on the roofs were coloured a shy night-blue. In the church, the radiant stained-glass slept in shades of grey. Only the street flowers growing in great round pots made use of the lamplight. Where the light touched them, their leaves shone dusky-green. Fuchsias, rhododendrons, impatiens and azaleas sprawled along the footpath and crept on to the road.

The children reached the harbour before Fabrice and the soldier arrived. The harbour was deserted but for dozing seabirds and themselves. They walked in single file along the sea wall, their arms held out for balance. They jumped down and ran to where the waves broke on the sand. They searched the night's blackness for the line where water met the sky. It was exciting to be alone on the beach, in the midst of a secret adventure. The children grinned at one another, and hid their mouths with their hands. Pascal swept the fishing net through the lapping waves. He caught a rope of seaweed and shook it off disgustedly. The toes of Coco's boots were wet, and frothed with white sea-foam: she felt herself sinking gradually into the pebbles and gritty sand.

The night was cool, and growing still. The candle-lit village behind them rested peaceably. For a time, the only sound they heard was the breaking of waves. The waves were tiny, scarcely more than ripples. Eventually Pascal spoke. "The Channel is calm. That's good."

"Monsieur Lieutenant won't get seasick," said Marcelle.

"Even if the Channel was very rough, he wouldn't get seasick." Coco felt it was important that her siblings understood this.

The sound of an approaching motorcycle made them turn and gaze. Coco took her hand from her pocket and reached for her sister's hand. Marcelle held the little paw tightly. They felt their hearts leap like birds.

For a moment they saw nothing but the high thin shops which lined up along the harbour. The street-lamps lit the shopfronts and cast ghosts across the glass. Then the motorcycle swept around a corner and its headlight washed over the shop awnings and balconies. Fabrice rolled the motorcycle to a halt while the children raced up the beach. "Lieutenant! Lieutenant!" they called, noisily as sparrows.

They met each other at the foot of the pier. The children could hardly believe that the soldier who lived in the woods was the same man who now stood on the pier. The soldier felt the children jump excitedly around him, and he wanted to laugh and cry. He wanted to go home, but he also wanted to stay.

"Shh!" cautioned Fabrice. "You'll wake the village!"

The children went repentingly silent, pressing their lips together. Coco and Marcelle took the soldier's hands. They followed Fabrice and Pascal down the pier. In the crook of one arm Fabrice carried a basket from which peeked bread and a flagon. In his hand he held the lamp. Cradled in his other arm was his time-worn violin.

The pier rasped woodenly under the footsteps of the five collaborators. Loose bolts lifted like shrugging shoulders, and sank back in their holes. Along the bolstered length of the pier were tied fishing boats of various kinds. Some were rangy craft, sporting lanky masts. Others were squat and bobbed in the water like weighty corks. The water sloshed heavily against the swollen hulls. The further along the pier they went, the more pungently the air smelled of brine. They heard the occasional splashing as sea-dwellers darted away. The breeze blew stronger as they walked further from shore, tossing Coco's curls round her face. The wind tweaked Fabrice's cap and knocked it from his head.

They had nearly reached the end of the pier when Fabrice finally stopped. He lit the lamp but kept the flame low. The soldier stared about, seeing almost nothing. The children, however, saw a stubby wooden boat which nosed the pier playfully, rocking from side to side. Its hull was brown and its square white cabin was trimmed in faded blue. Its name was painted on its rump – the boat was called the *Pearl*. Fabrice hoped that the *Pearl* was so unassuming that, at least for one night, nobody would notice it gone. "Here we are," he said. "We're ready, Lieutenant. We shouldn't linger too long."

The soldier suddenly didn't know what to do. He knelt down on the pier. The little girls clutched to him. He hugged first Marcelle, then Coco. "Thank you," he whispered.

"I hope your brother John gets well," said Marcelle.

The soldier said, "I will never forget how kind you've been to me, Marcelle."

Coco hung stubbornly around his neck. "I don't want you to go!"

"I must," the soldier told her. "You know I cannot stay. Remember how brave you are, my Coco."

She nodded and sniffed and clung to him. "Will you come back and visit us one day?"

"I will," the soldier promised. "When the war is finished, Coco. I'll come back and sit under the trees. Until then, I will always think of you. So I'll never leave you – not really."

Coco and Marcelle tried to smile. Their faces were damp with seaspray and farewell. The soldier turned to Pascal, and smartly saluted him. "I'm honoured to have met you, Pascal. Everything that happens tonight will happen because of you. You are heroic."

Pascal blushed to his ears. He liked the sound of that word, *heroic*. He immediately decided his mission in life would be to have lots of people calling him that admirable word. "Thank you, Lieutenant Shepard," he said. "Good luck, Monsieur."

Fabrice was waiting on board the *Pearl*. Though the water was calm and the winds favourable, there was no time to waste. It would take half the night for Fabrice and the soldier to cross the Channel, and half the night for Fabrice to sail home alone. By dawn the *Pearl* must be bobbing innocently at the pier as if it had been there and nowhere else all night. By dawn, the soldier should be sitting in a quiet corner of another land, waiting for the sun to rise and light the path that would lead him home. It was amazing to think that, while the village slept, the little boat would chuff across the sea and visit a different country.

The soldier was glad there wasn't time to dally. "Goodbye, children," he murmured. "Goodbye."

Fabrice reached out to him. The soldier took Fabrice's arm and gingerly stepped off the pier. He felt small guiding hands against his back. He imagined the hands looked like butterflies. Then he stood beside Fabrice on the scaly deck of the *Pearl*, and the three children stood together on the pier. He struggled to see them through blurred eyes. "Goodbye," he said once more.

Pascal unhooked the mighty rope that moored the

Pearl. He leaned his weight against the prow and heaved with all his strength. The boat moved silently away from the pier. Fabrice had decided not to light the boat's lamps or fire up its small engine until they had drifted some distance from shore. The *Pearl* moved sleekly through the water, drawn to the open sea. With no lamps to brighten her, the boat vanished quickly in the dark. Marcelle, Coco and Pascal stood watching it, long after it had disappeared.

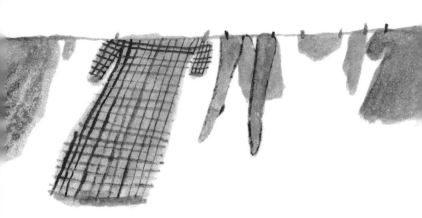

COCO IN THE WOODS

THE next day was Saturday. The children had to pay the dreadful price of the promise they'd made the night before. They had to do all their chores without one word of complaint. There was no time for them to go to the harbour to see if the *Pearl* was docked at the pier, or to run through the village to Fabrice's house and hammer at the yellow front door. Rather, sunrise saw Pascal beside his father at the dairy; Marcelle and Coco were imprisoned indoors,

helping their mother around the house. They helped wash the clothes, mop the floors, and polish the windows. They beat the rug and helped bake three loaves of bread. They were quite distracted, and were very glum. They kept forgetting to do things, or doing them wrong. They got under their mother's feet and were less assistants than pests. Their mother decided it would be easier to get the chores done without them. "It's a sunny day," she said. "Go and give Juliette a bath."

Bathing Juliette the pig was fun. Juliette loved to have the scrubbing brush scratched on her bald skin. She would poise like a ballerina, her snout tilted to the sky; her eyes would close with bliss as the water steamed on her. But even the prospect of bathing the pig did not lift Marcelle and Coco's gloom. Marcelle boiled the kettle and filled the bucket with soapy water.

Coco tethered Juliette to a post in the yard. Their shoulders were slumped as they did these things, their mood was not enthusiastic. They knew they should be happy that their soldier was nearing home, and they were happy; but they were also sorry for themselves. They felt that life would never again offer something so exciting as finding a soldier asleep in the woods.

Marcelle knelt beside the pig. She rolled up her sleeves. She applied the scrubbing brush to Juliette. The pig looked pleased, and seemed to smile. Coco squatted beside her sister. The sun was nice on the nape of her neck. A beetle on the cobbles was made alarmed by the splashes and dripping suds. Coco asked, "Where do you think he'll be now, Marcie?"

"I don't know," answered Marcelle. "Close to home, I suppose."

"I hope he can see the road properly. I hope he doesn't trip over. His eyesight was getting better. Do you think he'll see the road?"

"I don't know," said Marcelle.

Coco guided the beetle with her finger. It ran about in confused circles. "I wonder if the sea was rough? It looked smooth near the shore."

Marcelle didn't reply. She was scrubbing Juliette's flank. The pig snuffled, and wagged her head. Tidalwaves of water were flooding the cracks in the cobbles. The beetle scrambled for higher ground. "It didn't look rough in the harbour," mused Coco.

"Pass me the cloth," said Marcelle.

Coco passed the cloth. Marcelle sponged Juliette's prim face. Coco put her chin in her hands, squinting into the sunshine. Birds were darting here and there. Everything smelt summery. "I wonder what he'll do when he reaches home? He was going to take a bath. Maybe he's having a bath right now, just like you are, Juliette!"

"Shut up!" her sister snapped suddenly. "Don't say stupid things, Thérèse! Go away, I'm tired of you! Everything you say is stupid!"

Coco was shocked, and deeply hurt. Her eyes filled

and she skulked away down the lane. Marcelle, scowling, watched her go. She was sorry for scolding Coco, but glad to be left alone. She concentrated on making Juliette clean. She soaped the pig sternly. When her thoughts drifted she weighted them down with dragonflies and fruit flans and Émile Rivère. She thought about the polka-dot dress she hoped her mother would make for her. She thought about becoming a nurse, and bringing someone's medicine on a tray. She wanted to think about the soldier, but she wouldn't let herself. The soldier was gone; he wasn't coming back. Thinking of him would only make her cry. And Monsieur Lieutenant wouldn't like that – he'd want her to be happy. So Marcelle tried her hardest to think about things that made her happy.

Coco, however, was enjoying being mortally sad. She wandered down the lane sobbing woefully. She didn't dab away the tears that cascaded down her cheeks. "Lieutenant, Lieutenant!" she wailed. "Why – why – why?"

She supposed that anyone who saw her, a lonesome child staggering, weeping, along a lane, could not help but be touched by the poignancy.

She felt something crawling on her stomach and shrieked, dancing about and slapping herself frantically. A beetle dropped to the ground and lay capsized, its legs batting the air. It was the same beetle, Coco was sure, that had been in danger of drowning in Juliette's bath. Coco was impressed by its clever escape. She crouched down and gazed at it. Its carapace was black. Its head was a minuscule wedge with two waving nippers for teeth. Carefully Coco righted the creature onto its six feet. It commenced to trundle away calmly, as if nothing eventful had happened.

Coco sat back on her haunches. She had stopped crying. Her cheeks were wet, and she dried them on her dress. She glanced along the lane hoping no one had seen her bawling. She stood up and looked over the stone laneway wall. Beyond the wall were fields and, beyond them, the woods. Coco climbed the wall and jumped into the grass on the other side. "I'll find mushrooms for Juliette and cuckoo flowers for Marcie," she announced generously.

She roamed up the crest of a hill. She roamed down its other side. She marched through the long grass, plucking flowers here and there. She noticed some cows eyeing her. One bold heifer ambled closer, but bolted when Coco yelled, "Boo!" The sun was balmy and pleasing; she took off her socks and boots and left them sitting on a grey rock. She hoped she'd remember to find them again – then promptly forgot about them. The grass felt lovely between her toes. The earth was damp and cool. She strode on, humming dreamily. She tossed aside the flowers she'd picked for Marcelle. She could no longer be bothered with that.

Quite soon she was standing at the fringe of the woods. Coco tried to be surprised to find herself in the shade of the elms, but, inside, she knew that she'd been waiting all day to come here. The forest had been expecting her. Her lightheartedness dropped away and she became sombre. She stepped respectfully into the forest, as if into a cathedral.

"It's me," she said softly, walking through the shadows, hearing birds fly away. "It's only me, Monsieur."

The trees stood tall and peered loftily at her. Fallen twigs and leaves crumpled under her feet. She touched each tree as she passed it. The bark felt rough and cool. "It's me – Coco," she called. "Don't be frightened, Lieutenant, it's only me …"

A breeze in the treetops shook the leaves; some fluttered lightly down to her. Delicately Coco pushed aside branches of elder, holding her breath. There, ahead, was the hollow where the soldier had camped. There, stacked against his favourite tree, was a bundle of goods. With a tiny yelp of joy, Coco flitted across the earth. In her mind, the silver donkey leapt to life and ran to her.

She dived to her knees before the things the soldier had left behind. She rifled quickly through them. There was the pillow, the scarf, the woolly socks and

Papa's second-best shaving razor. Everything had been brushed clean and tidily folded. Coco squeezed the woolly socks and shook out the scarf. She investigated every atom of the pillow's feather stuffing. Her heart, which had been beating speedily, slowed down with disappointment. Ever hopeful, she searched again, flattening the pillow, plunging her hands in the socks. But the little silver donkey wasn't anywhere.

Coco sat back and stared peevishly at the ravaged goods. He'd left these things, but not the donkey. She couldn't help but feel aggrieved. She had so desperately wanted to keep the donkey. On the pier, she'd prayed he would make a gift of it to her. She'd imagined his brown hand reaching out to her, the glint of silver between his fingers. But he hadn't done it, and the boat had sailed away. Now the donkey was gone forever. Coco put her hands to her face and fought off waves of sorrow. *Be brave*, she commanded herself. The soldier had told her, on the pier, to remember that she was brave. Like Hazel had been, like the sky-donkey was, like the donkey with a hundred names: good and strong and brave.

A woodpecker rapped its beak against a tree. It made an empty, enticing sound. Coco peeked over her fingers in search of the bird. She glanced all around the clearing but couldn't see it. Her gaze returned to the pillow, the scarf, the razor, the socks. She wondered why the soldier had left these things here. He could easily have given them to Fabrice, who would have returned them safely.

Then, in a flash, she knew why. The soldier had left everything here because he had known Coco would come to the woods in memory of him, in search of the silver donkey.

… But the donkey wasn't here.

At least, Coco couldn't see it.

She frowned. She pouted. She rocked on her ankles, thinking hard.

The soldier had said that the donkey belonged to

the trustworthy and the brave. The soldier had said Coco was brave. She was trustworthy, too: she'd kept her promise and never told anyone about the soldier hiding in the woods.

The soldier's brother John said the donkey would remind its keeper to try their best. The soldier's brother John was a trustworthy and brave boy. It was he who had found the silver donkey, and given it to the soldier.

Coco sat up, blinking fast. "Oh!" she whispered.

She scrambled around the clearing on her hands and knees. She swept aside the twigs and stones that littered the forest floor. Very soon she discovered a patch of freshly turned soil. Fast as a rabbit, she began to dig. The dirt was black and heavy, but not hard to burrow through. The earth was loose in her fingers. The soldier had already dug for her.

It lay on its side, not very deep down. Coco snatched it up, shouting with laughter, and waved it in the air. She put it to her lips and kissed it. She cleaned it on her dress. She stared joyfully into its eyes. The little silver donkey shone back at her.

And somewhere on a beach far away, footprints crossed and were stamped from the sand as children ran about collecting seashells, laughing and playing in the sun.

SONYA HARTNETT was born in Melbourne, the second of six children. Her first book, *Trouble All the Way*, was written when she was just thirteen and published two years later. Since then she has gone on to write numerous successful novels, including *Thursday's Child*, winner of the 2002 Guardian Children's Fiction Prize; *What the Birds See*, which won the prestigious Age Book of the Year in Australia; *Stripes of the Sidestep Wolf* and *Surrender*.

Sonya says the plot of *The Silver Donkey* came to her after watching a TV documentary about the evacuation of Dunkirk. Soon after, she found a silver donkey in an antique shop. "When I held the trinket in my hand I knew I held the key to the book. It had never happened to me before, to see such promise and potential in an object. Later, while I wrote the book, I kept the donkey beside me: its physical presence seemed to suggest a reassuring reality behind the fiction. I hope *The Silver Donkey* will bring to a child somewhere the pleasure and wonder that children's books once brought to me. I hope it stays with them, that they remember it. Grandly, but most of all, I hope it plays some small part in making good people out of them – and through them, a good future to come."

LAURA CARLIN studied at the Royal College of Art and her work has featured in such publications as *Vogue*, *The New York Times* and the *Guardian*, as well as in publicity campaigns for Royal Mail, the London Symphony Orchestra and British Airways. She has won several awards, including the Sheila Robinson Drawing Prize, the Quentin Blake Award twice and the 2004 National Magazine Award. Laura says, "I loved being able to draw donkeys. And I had no trouble drawing the character of Coco. Her tantrums and sulks reminded me of myself at that age!"

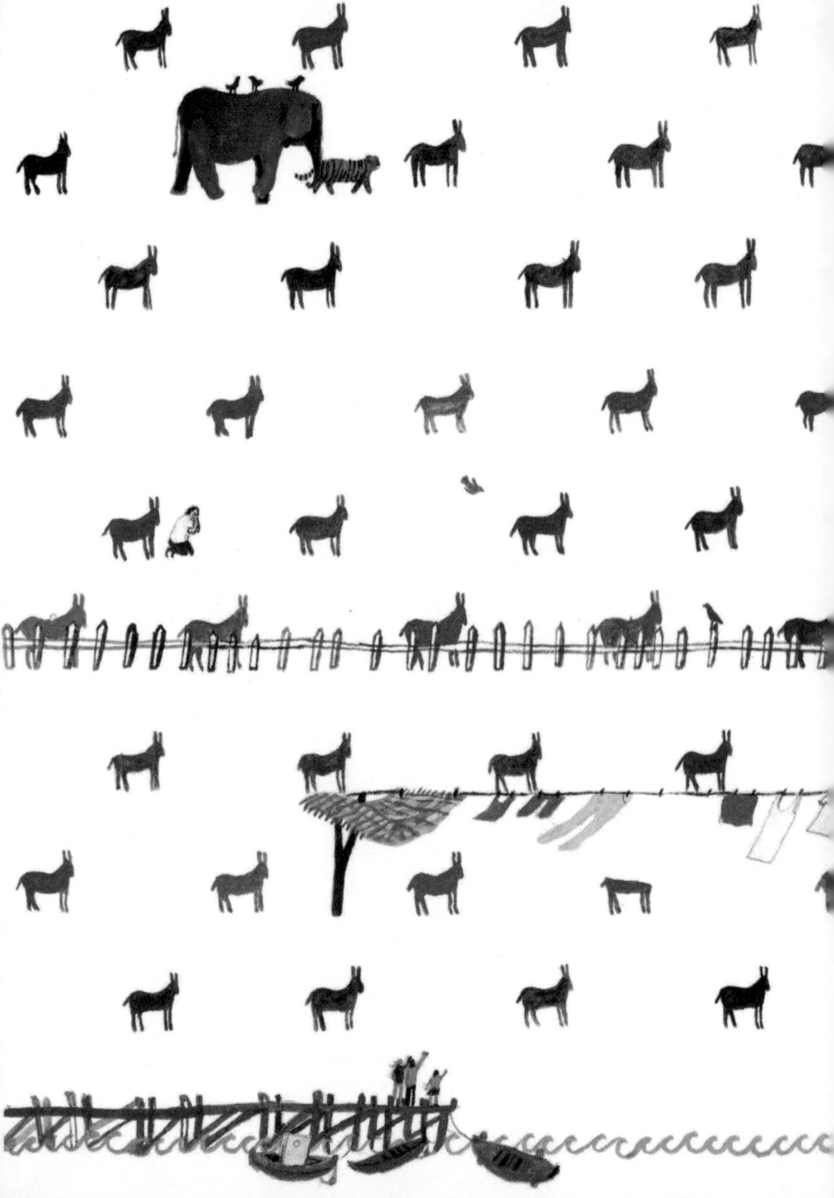